$\mathcal{P}$rince Albert stood in the middle of the road. If a car came around the bend now, the driver would never see him in time to stop.

"Move!" Taylor shouted full blast.

Prince Albert whinnied and turned his body toward her. As he did, a large white car drove into view, coming fast.

Prince Albert screamed as he reared high onto his back legs.

The car's horn blared, and then came the sickening sound of crunching metal.

Taylor was only dimly aware of her own anguished voice shouting.

*"No! No! No!"*

## Ride over to
# WILDWOOD STABLES

# WILDWOOD STABLES

## Learning to Fly

### BY SUZANNE WEYN

**SCHOLASTIC INC.**

New York   Toronto   London   Auckland
Sydney   Mexico City   New Delhi   Hong Kong

No part of this publication may be reproduced, stored in a retrieval system, or transmitted in any form or by any means, electronic, mechanical, photocopying, recording, or otherwise, without written permission of the publisher. For information regarding permission, write to: Scholastic Inc., Attention: Permissions Department, 557 Broadway, New York, NY 10012.

ISBN 978-0-545-14982-2

12 11 10 9 8 7 6 5 4 3 2          10 11 12 13 14 15/0

Printed in the U.S.A.          40
First printing, July 2010

With very special thanks to **Diana Gonzalez** for lending not only her expertise as a horsewoman, but also her creativity and literary skills to the creation of this manuscript.

# Chapter 1

Taylor Henry held Prince Albert's lead line casually in one hand as she walked the quarter horse down Wildwood Lane. The tree-lined country path leading in and out of Wildwood Stables was now vibrant with the rustling red, yellow, and orange hues of early autumn. Taylor could have easily ridden the black gelding on the dirt lane, but right then she preferred to be eye level with her horse.

They needed to have a serious talk.

"So, I know you love me. I love you just as much — more, even! But it can't just be you and me. I wish it could," she told him.

Prince Albert neighed. Lately, Taylor had noticed that whenever she spoke directly to Prince Albert he always made some noise in response. She loved that about him. It made her feel they were really communicating.

Taylor gazed into his soulful dark eyes and felt she heard him as clearly as if he'd actually replied aloud in words. He wanted to know why not. Why couldn't it just be Taylor and Prince Albert, without any other horses or riders?

"Because you have to be available for lessons and trail rides, that's why. And I need to work with the other horses." Taylor sighed in frustration. "It's part of our deal with Wildwood. Don't pretend you don't know all this. We've been through it a zillion times already!"

At this point Taylor was sure Prince Albert was simply being stubborn. It was mid-October, and he'd been living at the stable since the end of August. By now he had to understand that he couldn't be a one-girl horse.

Taylor had helped rescue him and his best pal, a cream-colored Shetland pony named Pixie, when they'd been abandoned by their owners. Against all odds, she'd even found them a good home here at Wildwood Stables. But the ranch could only afford to keep Prince Albert if he was a working trail and school horse. And, so far, he had not been at all cooperative.

"Sure, I know you've let Dana ride you," Taylor acknowledged. Dana was a seven-year-old girl with autism who had horse therapy sessions at the stable once a week. She would only work with Prince Albert, and to everyone's surprise, he allowed her on his back. They had even won a ribbon at a recent Rotary Club horse competition for kids with disabilities.

"And it's really great that you let her on; it's meant so much to her," Taylor continued. "But you have to do more. Being a two-girl horse is still not enough. Okay?"

A black SUV swung in very quickly from Quail Ridge Road at the end of the lane. It zoomed toward Taylor and Prince Albert as though the driver was completely unaware that a slim thirteen-year-old girl with long brown hair and a large black horse were standing in the path.

Startled by the car's speed, Taylor dropped the lead line and jumped back. Prince Albert reared in fright, neighing shrilly as his front two legs rose from the ground, kicking the air.

The glamorous blonde woman at the wheel of the SUV careened into a rapid curve to avoid the frightened horse in her path, but she made no effort to slow down. Beside the woman, a slim girl Taylor's age, also a blonde, watched the scene with unmistakable annoyance etched on her face.

Staggering backward, Taylor recognized the girl and the car just as the heel of her brown riding boot hit a tree root. Taylor fell on her butt, sending rockets of pain up her spine. As she scrambled to her feet, she couldn't stop to feel her injury, or even her fury at Plum Mason and her reckless mother.

Her entire attention was on Prince Albert, who was galloping in wild panic toward Quail Ridge Road.

Panting hard, heart thundering in her chest, Taylor raced down Wildwood Lane onto steep and curving Quail Ridge Road. Fast as she was running, it seemed to take forever to get there.

Taylor checked the field to her left. Some of Wildwood's other horses had been turned out and grazed there — but no Prince Albert.

Pivoting to her right, Taylor froze.

"Oh, no!" she shouted.

Up the hill, Prince Albert stood in the middle of the road, wide-eyed and bewildered. He was standing directly in the middle of a blind curve in the road. If a car came around the bend now, the driver would never see him in time to stop.

"Prince Albert! Prince Albert!" Taylor shouted in her most commanding tone.

Prince Albert swung his head around to her. His ears were back and flattened, a sign of his anxiety.

Taylor clapped her hands sharply. "Walk on! Move, Prince Albert! Now! Move to the other side! Get off the road!"

Prince Albert usually obeyed commands well. Why wasn't he moving?

His nostrils flared and his eyes were wide. He stood frozen in terrified confusion.

Clicking to the frightened horse, Taylor hurried up the hill toward him, deciding on another approach. "Come to me, boy. Come on." She worked to disguise the urgent fear in her voice, hoping he would calm down enough to respond.

It was no use! He wasn't budging.

"Move!" Taylor shouted full blast, clenching her fists as her cheeks reddened with the strain. Maybe she could at least startle him off the road.

At the sound of her agitated tone, Prince Albert whinnied and turned his body toward Taylor. As he moved, a large white car drove into view, coming fast.

Prince Albert screamed as he reared high onto his back legs.

The car's horn blared, and then came the sickening sound of crunching metal.

Taylor was only dimly aware of her own anguished voice shouting.

*"No! No! No!"*

## Chapter 2

Taylor stood on the side of the road beside a deputy sheriff with the name Michael Casey pinned under his badge. Her stomach knotted as she watched the emergency medical team that had arrived in a matter of minutes, sirens shrieking, carefully lift the two passengers from the white luxury car.

"I'm okay, really," a girl with long, nearly black hair told the emergency medical techs who were readying a stretcher for her. "Help my mother first."

Taylor wanted to rush to the girl's side, but the sheriff and EMTs had insisted she stay back, away from the crash. She managed to make eye contact with Wildwood's fourteen-year-old assistant junior barn manager, Mercedes Gonzalez, and tried to relay how awful she felt. Taylor was sure Mercedes was coming to work at the barn as she always did on Monday afternoons after school.

Mercedes shot Taylor a questioning glance. Clearly, she was still unsure of exactly what had happened.

Taylor understood her confusion. There was no reason Prince Albert should have been standing in the road — the Wildwood girls never rode out onto Quail Ridge. It was way too curving, steep, and dangerous.

Mercedes' elegant, dark-haired mother sat on the ground clutching her leg, obviously in great pain. Mrs. Gonzalez's white pantsuit had been showered with broken safety glass from the smashed front windshield. Her pants leg was ripped open, revealing a knee that was swollen and cut.

"It could be broken," a heavyset male EMT said to the petite redheaded female EMT working with him.

The front and right half of the white car was embedded in the trunk of a thick pine tree. The car had skidded off the road to avoid hitting Prince Albert and had crashed through the stone wall that ran alongside Quail Ridge Road. The ancient tree had been the only thing to stop the car from careening down the steep, wooded ravine beside the road.

"And you said your horse broke loose onto the road?" Deputy Casey asked, checking the story Taylor had already told him.

Taylor nodded. She'd met Deputy Casey before, though he gave no sign of remembering her. He was the same thirtyish deputy who'd said he'd have to take Prince Albert and Pixie to auction if Taylor and her mother's friend Claire Black — an animal rehabilitator — couldn't find the two equines a home. Claire knew Michael Casey from school, which meant he had grown up right there in Pheasant Valley.

"And where is your horse now?" Deputy Casey asked Taylor.

Taylor opened her mouth, but no sound came out. She shut her eyes and drew in a slow, unsteady breath, trying to calm herself enough to reply. "He jumped over the stone wall and ran down the ravine," she explained when she had regained her voice. "He was scared. I have to go find him right now. Can I go?"

"Was he injured?"

"I'm not sure." She wasn't certain if Mrs. Gonzalez

had swerved in time to avoid hitting Prince Albert altogether.

Taylor was dying to race off after her horse, but first she had to make sure Mercedes and her mother were all right. Now that she saw that their injuries weren't life-threatening — and that she wasn't being allowed to help them, anyway — she ached to find her horse.

"We'll send a team out to search for him," Deputy Casey told Taylor.

Icy fingers of panic ran up Taylor's spine. "You won't hurt him, will you?"

"Not unless he's a danger to anyone."

"A danger?" Taylor scoffed anxiously. "He's gentle and sweet. How could he endanger anyone?" In rural Pheasant Valley, the sheriff and his deputies sometimes "put down" injured or dangerous animals. "Putting down" was a gentle way of saying they would shoot the animal.

"If anything, Prince Albert is the one in danger," Taylor added.

The officer's eyes darted across the road to the smashed car and broken wall. His gaze lingered on Mrs. Gonzalez moaning in agony beside Mercedes, whose eye area was developing a nasty purple bruise.

"That wasn't his fault," Taylor insisted passionately. "A car sped past and frightened him."

"You were riding him out here on Quail Ridge?" Deputy Casey asked evenly but with an undercurrent of accusation.

"No!" Taylor told him once again exactly where she had been and what had happened.

"Why don't you come back to the ranch with me?" suggested Deputy Casey. "I'll need a statement from Mrs. Mason and her daughter."

"Can I please look for Prince Albert first?" Taylor pleaded.

"I'll call for a search party to look for him while we go to the ranch," Deputy Casey insisted.

Taylor glanced back at Mercedes, who was holding a cold pack to her nose and watching as they loaded her mother into the ambulance. "Is she okay?" Taylor called.

Mercedes shrugged dismally. "I'll let you know."

With a nod to Mercedes, Taylor followed Deputy Casey down the road to where a female officer sat in the driver's seat of a police car. "I've set warning flares along the road and called for a tow truck," she reported as Deputy Casey got into the passenger's seat beside her.

Taylor hesitated outside the vehicle. She had never been in a police car before, and she was scared to get in. "Climb in back," Deputy Casey instructed her from the front seat.

"Am I . . ." Taylor hesitated. What she was about to say might be stupid, but she had to ask anyway. Still staying outside the car, she spoke to the female deputy — noticing that her nameplate identified her as Connie Gomez — through her open window. "Am I . . . I'm not . . . under arrest or anything?" Taylor asked.

As Taylor spoke the words, the full weight of what had happened flooded through her.

She had let Prince Albert get away from her. Now he was lost, possibly injured.

Indirectly, she had been responsible for a car accident that had hurt Mercedes and her mother — had destroyed their car.

Was she in trouble — would Wildwood Stables be held responsible?

"You're not under arrest," Deputy Gomez assured

Taylor. "We just have to talk to the driver of the other car you told Deputy Casey about and to the owner of Wildwood Stables."

"Why do you have to talk to Mrs. LeFleur?" Taylor asked.

"She owns Wildwood, and the ranch could possibly be held responsible in a lawsuit by the driver or for endangering the public safety," Deputy Gomez explained. "It all depends on the circumstances. That's why we need the full story."

Taylor didn't know how she could face Mrs. LeFleur with this news. The ranch's owner had poured every cent she possessed and so many hours of effort into getting the ranch going. Now it might all be destroyed.

Suddenly, Taylor wished she *was* under arrest. At least if she were locked safely behind bars she could hide from the world.

# Chapter 3

$\mathcal{I}$ hope you're not saying this is my mother's fault!"

"Well, it sort of *is* what I'm saying," Taylor admitted to Plum Mason. "Your car nearly ran us right off Wildwood Lane."

Although Plum was Taylor's least favorite person on the planet — certainly the classmate at Pheasant Valley Middle School she most disliked — she couldn't remember ever loathing Plum more than she did at this moment. The girl had laughed in Taylor's face when she tried to explain why she'd lost control of Prince Albert.

Mrs. Mason, Plum, Mrs. LeFleur, Taylor, and the two deputies were assembled directly in the doorway of the ranch's red main building that housed the office, the tack room, and the six indoor stables.

When Taylor arrived with the deputies, Plum was just coming in from riding Shafir, the young chestnut Arabian mare with a white blaze down the front of her muzzle that she leased from Wildwood Stables. Plum was dressed for English-style riding in gleaming black knee-high boots and tan breeches. Diamond stud earrings shone when she tilted her head to the side, swinging her long, blonde hair around the shoulders of a cropped navy riding jacket. In her leather-gloved hand, Plum now held the velvet riding helmet she had just removed.

In Taylor's opinion, any claim Plum might have had on good looks was completely overshadowed by the haughty arrogance of her expression.

Plum stepped aggressively toward Taylor. "Well, what were you and your horse doing standing in the middle of the path? It's for cars! If you hadn't noticed, it's the only way in or out of the ranch."

A short brunette woman of around sixty, wearing jeans and a barn jacket, stepped between them. "Girls! Please!" Mrs. LeFleur interrupted, adjusting her thick glasses on her nose. She raked her hand anxiously through her tangle of short, unruly curls. "The situation is difficult enough without the two of you sniping."

Taylor glared at Plum, who returned her glowering expression. Taylor had been making an effort — for the sake of Shafir and the ranch — to be friendly to Plum. But today's events had changed that. There was no way she could ever again even fake a friendly face where Plum was concerned.

"Mrs. Mason, could you give us your account of what happened?" Deputy Casey requested.

"I'd be happy to," Mrs. Mason replied. "I was bringing Plum to the ranch so she could work with the horse she leases. Shafir is still somewhat wild, and Plum has been giving her much-needed training."

Taylor had to look away to keep the expression on her face from betraying her outrage at Mrs. Mason's words. Taylor, Mercedes, and Daphne Chang — the ranch's fifteen-year-old riding instructor — had been working hard to train the high-spirited Shafir. That the horse was progressing so well was due to *their* hard work and patience. Even more challenging was the constant monitoring they kept on Plum, to make sure she didn't hurt Shafir with her rough and domineering training style, her hard-driving riding, and her careless grooming.

"We were on our way into the ranch," Mrs. Mason continued, "when this girl and her horse suddenly appeared in our way."

"I did not *suddenly* appear," Taylor protested.

But Deputy Casey spoke before anyone paid attention to Taylor. "At that time was Taylor in control of the horse?" he asked Mrs. Mason.

"No, the horse was just walking there," Mrs. Mason replied.

"I had him on a lead line," Taylor objected, raising her voice so that this time she would not be ignored.

"If he was on a lead then how did he run off?" Plum challenged.

"He ran because *your mother* was *speeding* and almost hit him!" Taylor cried, furious. Only after the words came out did she realize she'd shouted them. But this was too much.

Plum and her mother were lying!

"Taylor!" Mrs. LeFleur scolded.

Taylor wheeled around to face Mrs. LeFleur. "Well, it's true!"

Mrs. LeFleur stared pointedly — even through the woman's thick glasses, Taylor could see the ranch owner's eyes widen — with an expression that ordered Taylor to calm down. The stable owner knew how much Taylor disliked Plum, and she was constantly advising Taylor to be more tolerant of her. Plum was a paying customer, someone the new ranch could not afford to lose.

"Were you speeding?" Deputy Casey asked Mrs. Mason.

"Definitely not. My SUV handles excellently, but if I'd been going too fast, I'd never have been able to avoid hitting the horse and the girl as I did."

"Were you aware that the horse had run off?" Deputy Gomez asked Mrs. Mason.

"Not at all. I would have stopped if I thought they needed help."

As Mrs. Mason continued telling the deputies how blameless she was in the incident, Taylor glanced over to the corral closest to the main building. Shafir was still saddled and prancing playfully. The expensive purebred

Arabian had been a gift from Mrs. Ross, the owner of the fancy Ross River Ranch. At first, Mrs. LeFleur had refused to accept the frisky young mare, wanting nothing to do with Mrs. Ross. Eventually, though, Taylor had convinced Mrs. LeFleur that the ranch needed Shafir, and Mrs. LeFleur had taken her in and leased her to Plum.

Taylor often wondered why Mrs. LeFleur disliked Devon Ross so much. She'd even searched for the answer online and come up with a shocking revelation — Mrs. LeFleur had been the matron of honor at Mrs. Ross's wedding to the son of a multimillionaire. Someday, Taylor would work up the nerve to ask Mrs. LeFleur about it, but until then, the relationship between the two women would remain a mystery.

Taylor watched as the Arabian mare picked up a stick that had fallen into the corral from the towering maple that stood on the other side of the fence. The stick blazed with the red leaves still on its branches, and it reminded Taylor of a cheerleader's bright pom-poms. Shafir bobbed her head up and down, trying to entice Pixie, the Shetland pony who was also in the corral, to chase her for the bright prize.

But Pixie would not be engaged in such a frivolous pastime. Unwilling to be distracted, Pixie turned her large head with its frizzy blond mane toward the ranch entrance. Taylor knew the pony was searching for her best friend, Prince Albert.

Before taking Prince Albert for their walk, Taylor had promised the devoted Pixie that they would be right back. To keep Pixie from following Prince Albert — as the pony always did, whenever Prince Albert went anywhere — Taylor had put both of them in the corral, and then led Prince Albert out, shutting the corral gate before Pixie had a chance to follow.

Taylor had felt badly about this trick but convinced herself it was for Pixie's own good. If they were both to be used for lessons and trail rides, they would have to be separated at times. Taylor told herself it was good training — a much-needed dose of tough love. Now, though, watching Pixie keep such a devoted vigil, waiting so steadfastly for her friend, just increased Taylor's awful feelings of guilt.

"Have the deputies found Prince Albert yet?" Taylor asked Deputy Casey.

Deputy Casey held up a finger, indicating that Taylor should wait a moment, and clicked on his two-way radio. "Any sign of the runaway horse?" he asked someone on the other end.

"Negative. Still searching," came the reply.

# Chapter 4

**W**hen Taylor was finally given permission to search for Prince Albert, she had raced up to Wildwood's open grazing pasture that sat at the top of a hill at the back of the ranch. She sometimes rode Prince Albert on a trail behind the pasture, and she was hoping he might be there.

Now she was weary from searching in the woods for more than two hours, and she settled down to rest on a low, flat boulder by a gurgling creek. She pulled out her cell phone and found the number she needed. "Hey, Daphne. Were you able to get through to Mercedes?" she asked when her friend picked up her cell.

"Yeah," Daphne confirmed. "She's okay. Her mother has a broken leg, though."

"Oh, man . . . I feel terrible."

"It wasn't your fault."

"In a way it was," Taylor disagreed. "I should have kept a better hold on Prince Albert, stopped him from rearing like that."

"Plum's mother shouldn't have been zooming down Wildwood right at you," Daphne countered.

Taylor pictured Daphne with her long, glossy black hair and slim, graceful elegance. A first-rate rider, Daphne would never have let something like this happen. Yet she was making sure Taylor knew she didn't think any less of her for this awful accident, and Taylor was grateful.

"How's Pixie?" Taylor asked.

"I'm using her for a lesson with Maddy. They're walking around the corral. The lesson seems to be distracting Pixie for now," Daphne reported. "Where are you?"

"I came down to the creek off the path in the woods behind our pasture," Taylor replied. "I was here with Prince Albert and Pixie a few times, and I know he likes to drink from the running water, but I don't see him."

Taylor had been so sure that if she just called to him, Prince Albert would hear her and follow the sound of her voice. Why wasn't he responding to her calls?

"Where could he be, Daphne? What if he wanders out on the road again and gets hit?" Taylor's voice cracked with fear as she spoke. "Maybe Mrs. Gonzalez hit him when she swerved and didn't realize it. What if he's injured? I couldn't stand it if anything happened to him."

"You'll find him. Don't worry. As soon as the lesson is done I'll saddle Mandy and come to help you search," Daphne said, referring to her gray, speckled barb quarter horse mare.

"Thanks. Call me when you're in the woods, okay?"

"Okay. Good luck."

Taylor stuck her phone into her back pocket and stood. Cupping her hands to her mouth, she called out, forcing her voice to its loudest: "Prince Albert! Come to me, boy! Prince Alllllllberrrrrrrt!"

A rustling in the bushes across the creek made Taylor whirl toward it.

"Don't get your hopes up. It's only me." The stocky, broad-faced boy emerging from the thick tangle of boxwood bushes was Travis Ryan, Taylor's best friend. Travis ran a hand along the top of his bristle of straight blond hair, knocking out stuck leaves and twigs. "I heard you calling, so I guess you haven't found him yet?"

Travis didn't ride but did repairs at the ranch, mostly because Taylor had persuaded him to help. Though he grumbled about it, Taylor suspected he secretly liked being there. Wildwood was an exciting new adventure and — usually — a fun place to be. Travis had showed up to fix a rung of the spilt-rail fence just as the deputies were leaving. When he heard what had happened, he'd instantly put down his toolbox and called Taylor in the woods, offering to help search.

Taylor replied with a dismal shake of her head, then threw her arms out in frustration. "Where could he be?"

"Did you check back at Wildwood?"

Taylor nodded. "Not there."

"He might wander home eventually."

"If he's not hurt and can find his way."

"Someone should check the pasture," Travis suggested.

"That would be great if he was there."

A tall, dark-haired boy of about fourteen appeared at the top of the slope. He had broad shoulders and wore a red-and-black-plaid shirt above jeans and cowboy boots.

"What's *he* doing here?" Travis grumbled.

"I guess he came to help," Taylor replied as she waved to Eric Mason, Plum's cousin.

"We don't need him," Travis remarked sourly. He eyed Eric with grim disapproval as the boy hurried down the wooded slope toward them.

"We need all the help we can get." Taylor worked to keep her voice neutral, not wanting to betray the excitement she felt every time she saw Eric. He was so good-looking and nice. Taylor didn't want to think of herself as having a crush — but her heart rate quickened whenever he showed up, and Taylor suspected she was babbling every time she spoke with him.

Eric had helped Taylor and the other girls learn horse games when Wildwood Stables ran a games event two weeks before. But he worked at Westheimer's Western Ranch on the other side of Pheasant Valley and went to a private school in Dobbs Ferry, which meant that Taylor didn't know when she'd see him again — if ever.

But here Eric was, and despite her worries over Prince Albert, Taylor was happy to see him.

It was weird, though, the way Travis always made her feel disloyal for liking Eric so much. It wasn't as if Taylor and Travis had ever acted like boyfriend and girlfriend. They'd been each other's best friends since elementary school, but it was never anything romantic. Not even close!

"Tell him to go away," Travis mumbled as Eric approached.

"Shh!" Taylor hissed sharply. "He'll hear you."

"So? I want him to."

"Shh."

Eric was nearly to them and waved. "I'm glad I found you. I thought that might be your voice calling. I guess you haven't found him, though."

"No, we found him. He's scuba diving in the creek," Travis said without a hint of smile.

Taylor jabbed Travis in the arm with her elbow. "No, we haven't found Prince Albert," she told Eric. "I suppose you heard about what happened from Plum and her mother."

Eric shook his head. "No, I was taking out a trail ride

over at Westheimer's, and I got a call from Carl to be on the lookout for Prince Albert. The sheriff called him. I came right over as soon as I could because I don't think he could have gotten all the way over to Westheimer's that fast."

"He *is* a horse," Travis pointed out snidely. "They're known for traveling rapidly over long distances."

Judging from Eric's narrowed eyes, Taylor knew he'd caught the sarcasm in Travis's tone, but then he obviously chose to ignore it. "I think it's more likely that he'd stay somewhere he was already familiar with, so I came to Wildwood. Daphne told me you were in the woods searching."

"Thanks for helping," Taylor said. "I figured the same thing. Prince Albert has been in these woods before, on trail rides with me. I even rode him and Pixie through here the first time I brought them from Claire's to the ranch."

"Who's Claire?" Eric asked.

But Taylor and Travis had turned to face each other, eyes wide. "Claire's!" they said, both at the same time. "What if he went back to Claire's house?"

Travis shook his head. "Wouldn't she have called, though?"

"Not if she's out and hasn't come home yet," Taylor disagreed. She began hurrying up the slope, waving for Travis and Eric to follow. "Come on. There's a path right near here that leads to her house."

"Who's Claire?" Taylor heard Eric ask again.

# Chapter 5

Taylor, Eric, and Travis came out of the woods into a field of tall grass. Across from the field was a circle of bungalow-style former summer homes that residents had winterized by adding insulation and heat. These dated back to the 1920s, when Pheasant Valley had been a vacation spot. There were several communities like this one peppered throughout the town, interspersed among the larger, newer houses.

"That's Claire's house on the end," Taylor said, pointing for Eric's benefit. Travis had been there many times before. Claire Black was Taylor's mother's best friend since forever; Taylor thought of her as an aunt. She was a county-registered wildlife rehabilitator, which meant that if a wild animal was injured or abandoned, the person who found the animal would give Claire a call. Sometimes the local sheriff would be the one to call Claire to go out on a rescue.

As they crossed the field, Taylor hoped Prince Albert would be waiting for her in Claire's driveway. She recalled the improbable way in which she had come to own Prince Albert and Pixie. It was hard to believe it had all happened just two months earlier, when Claire asked her to accompany her on a wildlife rescue.

Ever since Taylor was in elementary school, Claire had taken her along on wildlife rescues because she knew how much Taylor loved all animals. They'd once lured a capuchin monkey from a tree and, another time, trapped a baby alligator that had gotten into someone's basement. Mostly, though, they rescued deer that had been hit and badly injured by cars, or abandoned cats and dogs, sometimes domestic bunnies. Occasionally, a Canada goose on nearby Mohegan Lake would break a wing.

It was while out on a rescue call with Claire that Taylor had found Prince Albert and Pixie abandoned in a small barn. They'd been filthy and nearly starved. With no place else to take the neglected equines, they'd trailered them back to Claire's quarter of an acre, fenced-in front yard.

According to the animal laws in Pheasant Valley, you needed five acres of land to keep a horse or pony on private property. After a neighbor had called to complain, Deputy Casey had given Claire three days to find Prince Albert and Pixie a more suitable home before he took them to be sold at auction. Taylor immediately searched horse auctions online and learned — to her horror — that although selling horse meat was no longer legal in the United States, it was allowed in other countries. Agents from these countries often bought horses for this purpose at auctions.

Fortunately, Taylor heard about Wildwood Stables and had the great good fortune of convincing Mrs. LeFleur to take Pixie and Prince Albert in as working school horses. From that day up to now, Taylor had thought her biggest problem was that Prince Albert wasn't agreeable to letting just any rider on his back. He only wanted Taylor, and then, slowly, fragile, autistic little Dana. But no one else.

Taylor smiled unhappily as she thought of all this. That problem seemed so small and manageable compared to losing Prince Albert altogether.

An elderly woman in a long winter coat, her hair covered with a knit cap, strode down the driveway of one of the houses behind a small white dog on a leash. She crossed the road and entered the field. It was Mrs. Kirchner, who had once been Taylor's teacher at Pheasant Valley Elementary. She was one of the crankiest teachers Taylor had ever had, and she was the neighbor who'd called the sheriff's office about Prince Albert and Pixie.

"Taylor Henry! Travis Ryan! Why aren't you two in school?" Mrs. Kirchner scolded when she noticed Taylor, Travis, and Eric.

"It's Saturday," Taylor reminded her.

"Oh, yes. Of course it is," Mrs. Kirchner mumbled.

Taylor figured that if the woman had seen Prince Albert around, she'd certainly mention it, so there was no reason to ask.

"Do you still have that pesky horse and pony down at Wildwood Stables?" Mrs. Kirchner inquired.

Taylor looked at Eric and Travis with surprised eyes

before turning back to Mrs. Kirchner. "You know about Wildwood Stables?"

"Of course I do!" Mrs. Kirchner snapped. "I've lived in Pheasant Valley for over sixty years! Wildwood Stables was practically the center of the town back when I was a girl. The place was run by the Moore family for generations."

*Moore?* Taylor had recently come across someone with that name. But where? She couldn't remember.

"Did you ever go there?" Travis asked.

"No, but my youngest sister was friendly with Bernice Moore."

"You mean LeFleur," Eric corrected her.

Mrs. Kirchner shot him a withering glare. "I know what I mean, young man. Bernice *Moore* grew up on the ranch with her aunt and uncle and her cousin, Devon Moore."

Taylor suddenly recalled where she'd heard the name. Of course! She had seen it online when was researching the connection between Mrs. Ross and Mrs. LeFleur.

Before she'd married Harrison Ross, Mrs. Ross's name had been Moore, Devon Moore.

Taylor had never known Mrs. LeFleur's unmarried

name, but according to Mrs. Kirchner, it was also Moore!

Mrs. LeFleur and Mrs. Ross were related!

But Mrs. LeFleur seemed to hate Mrs. Ross so much!

"Bernice Moore's father and mother died together in a plane crash," Mrs. Kirchner continued. "The Moore brothers had run the ranch together until that tragedy. Then Bernice went to live with her aunt and uncle. She and Devon were like sisters."

What could have happened?

"Did they fight?" she asked Mrs. Kirchner.

"How would I know?" Mrs. Kirchner snapped. "I don't have time to stand here gossiping with you. Get to school this instant!"

The bright, dancing amusement in Travis's blue eyes almost made Taylor burst out laughing, but she controlled herself. "All right, Mrs. Kirchner. Thanks," Taylor said as she moved on, with Eric and Travis following.

"What an old crank," Eric commented when they were out of earshot.

"Tell me about it!" Taylor agreed. "Try having her for a teacher like Travis and I did! It was horrible. But I can't believe she knew about Wildwood."

"Yeah, Mrs. LeFleur and Mrs. Ross are cousins!" Travis remarked. "Who would have guessed *that*?"

"Not me," Taylor said.

"They don't like each other?" Eric asked.

"Mrs. LeFleur doesn't like Mrs. Ross, that's for sure. I'll tell you about it another time," Taylor promised. "Right now I want to find out if Prince Albert is here."

Taylor led them up Claire's dirt driveway. To the left was a yard circumscribed by a split-rail fence wrapped in chicken-wire fencing. Six dogs of different breeds and sizes that Claire was boarding after rescuing them barked playfully. "Pipe down," Taylor told them pleasantly but firmly. At the sound of her command, the dogs all quieted. It was what Claire always said in her effort to keep the barking to a minimum for the neighbors.

Taylor was instantly disappointed that she didn't see Prince Albert there. If he had been, she'd have spotted him right away.

"Hey, Taylor," a woman's voice greeted her.

Turning toward the sound, Taylor saw Claire crouching over a large cardboard box. She was a petite woman in her forties with chestnut hair cut to her chin.

"Hi, Claire," Taylor returned the greeting as she walked over and peeked into the box. Inside, a mother cat lay on her side contentedly while four kittens suckled. "Ahh," Taylor crooned fondly, bending forward for a closer look. Then she jumped back in surprise. "Those aren't kittens!" she cried.

Claire laughed. "No, they're raccoon kits. The cat's kittens died from the cold last night, and the raccoon babies lost their mother when she got hit by a car. Someone heard the raccoon babies crying in the stump of a tree and called me. It worked out perfectly, since I had just picked up Mama Cat, who was still producing milk."

"She doesn't seem to mind feeding them," Travis observed as he and Eric came up alongside Taylor.

"No, she's happy to do it," Claire agreed. "Not all species can feed each other's babies, but cats and raccoons can."

Taylor introduced Eric to Claire and then explained what had happened.

"Oh, dear. That's awful," Claire sympathized, standing. "Try calling the ranch again. Maybe Prince Albert is back by now."

"That's right," Eric said. "I forgot until now, but I've heard that most of the time a horse on the loose will run home."

Taylor reached into her back pocket for her phone, but its tone sounded before she even reached it. "It's Mercedes," Taylor told the others once she'd checked the number readout. She clicked onto the call. "Hi, Mercedes. Where are you?"

On the other end of the call, Mercedes began to say something and then broke down sobbing.

# Chapter 6

Taylor sat in the back of Claire's van between Eric and Travis, her cell phone to her ear. "Well, tell her you have to be allowed to come to the stable. You're the assistant junior barn manager. We need you."

Mercedes sniffed. "Maybe she's just upset, and she'll change her mind later. They're putting a cast on Mom's leg right now, and that can't be fun." She burst into tears once more. "Wildwood is the only good thing that's happened to me since we came to Pheasant Valley. I don't know what I'd do if . . . if . . ." Mercedes started crying even harder than before.

"Is she all right?" Eric asked.

"Not really," Taylor replied, and she held her phone to him so he could hear Mercedes' sobs.

Eric cringed. "I guess not."

"Is that crying I hear?" Travis asked. "I can't picture Mercedes crying."

Taylor knew how he felt. Mercedes was efficient and no-nonsense when it came to horses and running the stables, so much so that she could even be annoyingly bossy at times.

"What's she so upset about?" Eric asked.

Taylor covered the phone. "Her mother said she's never allowed to come back to Wildwood again," she explained.

The three of them stared at one another as the impact of this hit them. The barn meant everything to Mercedes. She'd just moved to Pheasant Valley in her freshman year of high school and seemed to have no friends except for Taylor and Daphne, who only hung out with her there at the stables.

"Does she want us to come pick her up?" Claire asked from the driver's seat, tilting her head back toward Taylor.

Taylor passed Claire's offer along to Mercedes.

"No . . . wait, yes," Mercedes answered. "I'll call you. I don't think Mom will be able to drive home with a cast on her leg. We might need a ride."

"Are you all alone?" Taylor asked. "Did your dad arrive yet?"

There was silence on the other end.

"Is your dad there?" Taylor repeated.

"Uh . . . no. He's not going to be able to get here, I'm pretty sure of that." Taylor had never heard Mercedes mention her father, though she'd just assumed she had one. Suddenly, she wondered if she'd said the wrong thing.

"We'll wait there with her," Claire suggested.

"No, you'd better not," Mercedes said, having heard Claire for herself. "Mom thinks of you guys as belonging to Wildwood, and she's pretty mad at the ranch right now."

"*Pretty* mad?" Taylor questioned hopefully. Pretty mad didn't sound *too* awful.

"Really, *really* mad," Mercedes corrected. "Furious."

"Oh," Taylor said, and a sick lump of anxiety formed in the pit of her stomach.

*   *   *

Heading uphill toward the pasture, Taylor hurried behind Mrs. LeFleur. Wildwood's owner wore a barn jacket and hiking boots. The late morning sun glinted off her thick glasses. Eric and Travis walked several paces behind, neither one speaking to the other.

"I'm really so sorry about this, Mrs. LeFleur," Taylor said for what she knew was probably the tenth time that day. "Are you angry with me?"

Mrs. LeFleur had been incredibly generous to Prince Albert and Pixie by letting them board at Wildwood Stables in exchange for using them as school horses and for Taylor's work at the barn. Taylor was more grateful than she could say, and now she'd done something that possibly threatened the whole future of the barn. "I wish I could just rewind time," she added.

Taylor studied the stable's owner. Her glasses made it hard to read her expression. Mrs. LeFleur was not wearing her usual pleasant expression, though. That much was easy enough for Taylor to see.

"Taylor, if you *could* rewind, what would you have done differently?" Mrs. LeFleur asked. Her voice was not warm.

Taylor thought for a moment. "Should I have been

closer to the side of Wildwood Lane?" Honestly, she couldn't think of any way in which this was really her fault. It was Plum's mother who'd careened down the lane at top speed, but some instinct told Taylor that putting the blame off on the Masons wasn't the answer Mrs. LeFleur was after.

Mrs. LeFleur kept walking purposefully toward the pasture, but she turned her head to look directly at Taylor. "How about this? You should *not* have been on Wildwood Lane with a horse. It's too close to the road, and you should have known that."

The words *That's not fair!* rushed to Taylor's lips, but she didn't let them free. No one had ever told her not to take a horse onto the lane.

"What were you doing out there, anyway?" Mrs. LeFleur asked.

"Talking," Taylor replied meekly, "to Prince Albert."

"Talking!" Mrs. LeFleur echoed, incredulous. "You were having a conversation with Prince Albert that was so private you had to go out onto the lane to have it?"

"I thought he'd listen better if we could be alone," Taylor explained, suddenly feeling too stupid for words.

Mrs. LeFleur shook her head. The exasperated gesture made Taylor sure that Mrs. LeFleur *was* angry, and worse, disappointed in her. Taylor could feel her eyes begin to well up.

"I'm sorry, Mrs. LeFleur," she repeated, this time with an unsteady quaver in her voice. "I just didn't think he would ever bolt like that."

Mrs. LeFleur handed Taylor a clean though crumpled tissue from the pocket of her jacket, and the angry set of her expression softened a bit. "Stop apologizing, and let's find Prince Albert," she said more kindly. "He's got to be up here somewhere. Prince Albert thinks of this as his home by now, and I just think he would come back here."

"Unless he's lost," Taylor worried.

"Possibly," Mrs. LeFleur allowed, "but horses are good about finding their way home."

They arrived at the pasture gate, and Taylor held it so Mrs. LeFleur and the two boys could pass through, then she relatched it. In the field, Daphne Chang sat on her speckled gray mare, Mandy. The fifteen-year-old riding instructor waved when she saw them come into the pasture.

Taylor took a moment to admire how relaxed and at ease Daphne appeared on her horse. One of Taylor's goals was to someday be as excellent a rider as Daphne. It might take a long time, but Daphne was helping Taylor learn more about horses and riding, and Taylor felt she couldn't ask for a better teacher.

"Daphne, is Prince Albert up here?" Mrs. LeFleur called as Daphne and Mandy approached them, passing Cody, a broad-chested white gelding with black spots, a purebred Colorado Ranger.

But even before Daphne could reply, Taylor already knew Prince Albert wasn't there. The sure sign was that Pixie had positioned herself at the pasture gate. Her fuzzy, thick tail flicked from time to time with agitation, and her eyes scanned the landscape, keenly alert for the return of her dear friend, Prince Albert.

Taylor was reminded again that the closeness of Pixie and Prince Albert was another knotty problem that needed to be straightened out. Wherever Prince Albert went, Pixie followed — and if she couldn't, she became extremely anxious and depressed.

Taylor separated from the group and approached Pixie. "Where did he go, girl?" she asked as she stroked the aged pony's frizzed mane. Almost as if she understood the question, Pixie gazed into Taylor's eyes. Her ears swiveled forward suddenly, and she raised her head, seeming to detect a scent on the crisp autumn breeze.

"Is it Prince Albert, Pixie?" Taylor asked. "Is he nearby?"

Eric and Travis joined Taylor, while Mrs. LeFleur spoke with Daphne several yards away. "I think she senses him somewhere," Taylor told them.

"How could you tell?" Travis asked.

Eric spoke before Taylor got a chance to reply. "Her ears are forward, which means she finds something interesting, and look how she's sniffing the air. Whatever she smells has got her full attention."

"I could see *that*," Travis said in an annoyed voice. "I'm not an idiot."

Despite her concern for Prince Albert, Taylor turned away as if searching for her horse, but really she was disguising the fact that a smile — prompted by Travis's outburst — threatened to break loose on her face.

Travis knew almost nothing about horses, and she was sure he hadn't picked up any of the clues that Eric just mentioned. The only reason he helped out at the stable was because he and Taylor had been best friends since grade school. Now that Taylor was spending so much time at the barn, it was the best way for them to continue to spend time together. Travis didn't even ride and had no desire to learn. What he'd just said was a complete lie.

But Taylor understood why he'd said it. Travis thought Eric was a show-off because he went to the fancy Johnson School in Dobbs Ferry, even though he was on scholarship. Having Eric, who was an excellent rider, explain horse stuff was obviously more than Travis could stand. If Taylor had told him the exact same things, he wouldn't have minded at all.

Travis shot Taylor a look that she could read loud and clear: *There goes Mr. Show-Off-Know-It-All again.* She looked away, trying to pretend she hadn't caught the silent communication.

The truth was that Taylor felt lit up inside when Eric was around, especially if they were just talking to each other without anyone else in the conversation. She could just tell by the way he smiled at what she said that he thought she was funny and smart, which made her feel so great because she'd never thought of herself as being either of those things. He had already mentioned in passing that he'd described her to someone as "cute." She'd stood in front of the mirror for days afterward searching for previously unnoticed signs of cuteness. After a while, she could almost see what he saw. Sort of.

And she sure felt the same about him.

He was at the Johnson School on scholarship, after all — which proved he was a brain. And he had a sly, quiet sense of humor that she totally got. But that wasn't really what Taylor cared about. She couldn't completely nail down an exact reason why she fizzed inside when Eric was around — it wasn't something logical, it just happened.

Pixie turned from the fence and began walking toward the wooded area at the far end of the pasture. Taylor, Eric, and Travis hurried along at her side.

"Where are you going?" Mrs. LeFleur called to them.

"We're following Pixie," Taylor shouted back. "Maybe she knows where Prince Albert is."

From her gestures, Taylor saw that Mrs. LeFleur was telling Daphne to take Mandy and go with them.

What if they did find Prince Albert, and he was hurt? Having someone on horseback who could get help fast would be useful. Besides, Daphne was lively but calm, and Taylor felt better just knowing she was there.

As they followed Pixie into the woods, Taylor wished Pixie had been wearing a halter. It would have given her something to hold on to. Pixie was not likely to run away, but she'd thought that about Prince Albert, too. It seemed as though this was a bad luck day when anything could go wrong.

They traveled quietly together down a dirt path in the woods. Taylor had ridden Prince Albert this way with Pixie trailing behind. She knew there was a creek just ahead, and she could already hear its rushing water.

The multicolored leaves rustled above them, and sunlight dappled through the branches, forming wavering patterns of light on the ground. Occasionally, a bird's wild call or the snapping of a twig as squirrels scurried through the trees broke the steady, wavelike noise of the leaves.

"Maybe Prince Albert was trying to run home, but he got confused in here," Daphne suggested as she rode Mandy alongside Taylor.

Taylor looked around at the rise and fall of the hilly

landscape with its seemingly endless vista of trees. Prince Albert had only been here a couple of times before. "You could be right," Taylor agreed, and the idea gave her new hope. It made total sense. Taylor glanced at Pixie. "Is Prince Albert around here, girl?" she asked.

Picking up her pace, Pixie got ahead of the group. Taylor hurried to keep up with her.

"Does she smell Prince Albert or something?" Travis asked.

"I don't know," Taylor replied with a note of excitement in her voice.

"She can hear the creek and might only want water," Eric suggested.

Pixie was getting farther and farther ahead of them. Taylor was tempted to call her to halt, but she resisted, not wanting the pony to lose Prince Albert's scent if that was, in fact, what she was following.

"I'll stay with her," Daphne offered. With a gentle pressure to Mandy's sides, she moved her horse into a trot and was quickly beside Pixie.

Taylor watched anxiously as Pixie made a left turn off the path, headed toward the creek. Daphne and Mandy stayed right behind her. Daphne said something, but

Taylor couldn't quite make it out. "Did you guys hear what Daphne just said?" Taylor asked the boys.

"I think she said, 'There you are,' " Travis replied.

"That's what it sounded like," Eric agreed.

Taylor was instantly running down the path. *There you are* could only mean one thing. Veering left, she headed down the embankment. Her sneakers dug into the dirt, and she abruptly stopped when she realized Daphne was lifting her arm, signaling her to stop.

At the bottom of the embankment, Daphne and Mandy stood beside Pixie on the near side of the creek. Prince Albert was there on the far side.

Pixie neighed shrilly, throwing her head back and shaking her blond mane, calling to her friend to join them.

Prince Albert snorted in response but stayed where he was. Taylor's heart soared with relief. Then she noticed a clump of tall grass in front of Prince Albert. The black gelding's ears were forward with keen interest as he jutted his muzzle toward it. Daphne and Mandy also appeared riveted on the spot.

What were they all looking at?

# Chapter 7

Taylor approached slowly, creeping forward with silent caution. A twig snapped behind her, and she glanced over at Eric and Travis to her left. *Sorry*, Travis mouthed.

Inside the mound of high grass, she could see a dark form move just a little, a mere twitch, a flicker. It had to be some kind of animal sitting there very quietly. Was it injured? Why was Prince Albert standing next to it like that?

Coming alongside Pixie, Mandy, and Daphne, Taylor gazed across the stream but couldn't see more deeply into the mound. "Climb up with me," Daphne whispered, taking her foot out of her stirrup.

Taylor slid her boot into the empty stirrup and swung up behind Daphne. From this higher vantage point, she could look down into the grass, and immediately she let out a sharp gasp. "A fawn," she breathed in awe.

The small creature lay in the grass with its spindly legs folded. Its ears drooped at the tops, and the wet blackness of its nose glistened. White spots speckled its brown and gray coat. Deer were plentiful in Pheasant Valley and roamed freely, but Taylor had never before seen a baby this small. "It's *sooo* cute," she crooned tenderly.

"Why is Prince Albert standing there?" Travis wondered aloud as he came beside Mandy.

Daphne quickly shushed him.

"A fawn," Taylor whispered as softly as she could. "It's in the grass."

While Travis and Eric stretched high, standing on their toes in an attempt to see the little animal, Taylor dismounted and went to the edge of the creek. She clicked gently for Prince Albert to come to her.

The large black horse hesitated, glancing over at the fawn as though reluctant to leave it.

"The fawn will be all right," Taylor coaxed. "You can

come to me." Mentally, she was already mapping a path of rocks she could hop across the creek if Prince Albert wouldn't wade in on his own accord. She knew some horses were afraid of water, and though Prince Albert had never shied from drinking in the creek, she couldn't be sure if he'd be willing to cross through it.

But Prince Albert stepped right into the bubbling, crystal flow of the creek without hesitation. Taylor felt herself swell with pride as she always did when he displayed his calm and brave nature.

Taylor let the full force of her happiness and relief at finding her horse finally hit her. He wasn't hurt, and he had come right to her. Smiling broadly, she blinked back a quick impulse toward happy tears.

When Prince Albert stepped up out of the creek, Taylor rushed to his side and stretched her arms around his neck, laying her head against it. "I'm so sorry, boy, so sorry," she murmured emotionally, filled with remorse that she'd let anything bad happen to him. All she'd ever wanted for Prince Albert and Pixie was to give them a better life than the one they'd known before she and Claire had rescued them.

Pixie was quickly at their side. Her joy at being

reunited with Prince Albert was easy to see in the small and joyful dance she did, stepping from side to side and then back again. Her happy whinny made them all smile.

"Let's see the fawn," Travis suggested. He was already out in the creek, balanced on a low, flat rock rising just above the water.

"We should probably leave it alone," Daphne disagreed as she swung her legs to the ground in a graceful dismount. "Isn't that what they say to do?"

"I think so," Eric said. "The mother goes out to look for food and hides the baby away until she comes back."

Taylor was impressed with Eric's knowledge, but Travis shot her a look that she could read loud and clear: *There he goes again.* She looked away and pulled her cell phone from the front pocket of her jeans to call Claire. "We have Prince Albert," she reported when Claire answered. "We also found a little fawn in the woods."

Claire asked if it was injured, and once Taylor told her that she didn't think so, although she couldn't be sure, Claire instructed Taylor to leave the fawn where it was, saying that its mother would return for it. "Are you sure?" Taylor questioned. "It's really small, and Prince

Albert acted like he was standing guard over it or something."

Just as Daphne and Eric had said, Claire insisted that they should leave the fawn and come back to the ranch. She said the sky was becoming overcast. Looking up into the spaces between the leaves, Taylor saw that the bright blue had turned gray.

Mandy whinnied anxiously and shifted from side to side. "Rain," Daphne explained. "Mandy can sense a storm hours before it arrives."

"That's what Claire said, too," Taylor reported.

"Let's get out of here, then," Travis said. "Are you going to ride Prince Albert out, Taylor?"

Taylor shook her head. "I rode him bareback once in Claire's yard, but just at a walk. I wouldn't feel confident enough to do it on this uneven ground."

"I agree. It's too dangerous," Daphne said. "Do you mind if I ride ahead on Mandy? I want to bring Cody in from the pasture if it's going to rain and make sure Plum brings Shafir in and grooms her properly." She looked to Eric. "No offense, but your cousin loses interest once she's finished riding, and it's not good for the horse. I hope you don't mind me saying it, Eric."

Eric rolled his eyes. "You don't have to tell me how Plum is," he said. "I grew up around her."

*Poor you*, Taylor wanted to comment but held back. Eric and Plum *were* cousins, after all, even though they were in no way alike. He could say things about his cousin that maybe he wouldn't want to hear anyone else say.

"I know what a pain she can be," Eric added, "but, you know, she has her moments."

"What kind of moments?" Daphne asked as she remounted Mandy.

"You mean moments when she's not howling at the full moon?" Travis suggested snidely.

"No," Eric insisted in an annoyed voice that made Taylor happy she'd kept her mouth shut. "Moments when she's almost kind of human. Not often, but every once in a while."

"Yeah, I'm sure even The Joker has his good days," Travis remarked. His reference to the archvillain in *Batman* made Taylor smile softly. Travis loved his superhero comics and graphic novels almost as much as she loved horses and ponies.

"Plum's all right," Eric muttered, to which Travis snorted disdainfully. Taylor knew now she'd been right.

There was family loyalty there between Eric and Plum, despite the fact that Eric saw Plum clearly.

Once they had gone up the embankment, Taylor leading Prince Albert with Pixie close behind, they were back on the leaf-covered forest trail. "See you," Daphne said, clicking softly to Mandy and, leaning slightly forward in the saddle, cantering away.

Taylor became aware of rain tapping on the leaves around and above. "We'd better hurry," she said.

As she began leading Prince Albert and Pixie down the trail, Travis came alongside her on the right. "Do you think Mercedes' mom will really stop her from coming to Wildwood?" he wondered.

"I sure hope not," Taylor replied. "Mercedes loves it here."

"Would you miss her?" Travis asked.

"You know, it's weird, but I would," Taylor said. Mercedes and she hadn't gotten off to the best start when they'd first met two months earlier. Taylor found Mercedes almost unbearably bossy, and Mercedes had jumped to the conclusion that Taylor was responsible for the terrible condition of Prince Albert and Pixie. "Sometimes it still makes me mad when she tries to tell me what to do, but she does know a whole lot about horses, much more than I do. I've sort of gotten used to her, and I even like her, I guess. I *would* miss her."

"Mrs. LeFleur would have to find a new barn manager, too," Travis added.

"I could do it," said Eric, standing to the left of Prince Albert.

"What do you mean?" Taylor asked.

"You work at Westheimer's barn," Travis said, speaking at the same time as Taylor. "You can't work here, too."

"I got laid off. Ralph is having money troubles, and he had to let me go."

"Mrs. LeFleur doesn't pay us, at least not in money," Taylor told him. "I volunteer because she boards Prince Albert and Pixie in exchange for my work, and for using them for lessons and trail rides. Daphne gets paid by her lessons customers, and Mercedes does it because she used to have horses when she lived in Connecticut, and I think she just misses being around them."

"Why doesn't she get a horse here?" Eric asked.

"I don't know," Taylor admitted. "She's kind of secretive about her life, but I have the feeling her family used to be rich and then something bad happened. It's as though living here in Pheasant Valley is some big step down from the way things used to be for her."

"Have you ever been to her house?" Travis asked. "That would tell you if she's still rich."

Taylor shook her head. "Her mother drives a fancy car, though."

"Used to," Travis corrected.

Taylor cringed, hunching her shoulders. "You should have seen how crunched up that nice car was."

From somewhere in the distance a rifle shot rang out. Then another one blasted, sounding a bit closer.

Neighing anxiously, Prince Albert widened his eyes, flattened his ears, and flung his head back, startled by the sudden sound. "Settle down, boy," Taylor commanded with firm gentleness. "You'll scare Pixie."

Taylor, Eric, and Travis looked at one another. "We're idiots," Travis said suddenly. "Do you know what that was?"

Before Taylor could answer, her cell phone sounded, alerting her to a text message. It was from Claire.

GET OUT OF THE FOREST. HUNTING SEASON.

# Chapter 8

Taylor set Prince Albert's foot down and wiped the hoof pick she'd used to clean out his four hooves. Normally, she liked to groom him outside, but the rain had been pounding down so relentlessly that she'd been forced to bring Pixie and Prince Albert inside the enclosed stable.

Wildwood had six indoor box stalls, three on one side and three on the other. All six faced either side of a wide center aisle. Behind the ones on the right, there were three more. Their doors were not enclosed but looked out onto one of the ranch's three paddocks. Prince Albert was in the last stall on the right, and Pixie was next to him. Shafir, the chestnut Arabian mare that Plum leased, was across from Prince Albert, and Mandy faced Pixie.

Cody, the black-spotted, white Colorado Ranger gelding with the black-and-white mane and tail, was being boarded there and faced an empty stall.

At the end of these stalls was the main office on one side, across from the tack room. Outside the office hung a large bulletin board that listed everything happening at Wildwood Stables. It reported when everyone was scheduled to work, all the lessons and therapeutic riding sessions, and times when horses could be taken out on trail rides.

Mrs. LeFleur organized everything with amazing efficiency, which wasn't really that surprising considering that she had grown up at Wildwood before moving away for many years. She had returned only recently after inheriting the ranch several months earlier.

She wouldn't ride — Taylor wondered if that was because her son had been thrown and badly hurt, at least so she'd heard — but Mrs. LeFleur certainly knew how to run a horse ranch.

Daphne had groomed and fed Mandy and Cody before leaving for the day. Travis and Eric had helped Taylor clean up, but then they had also left.

After grooming Pixie and settling her into her stall,

Taylor was now working on Prince Albert in the center aisle. She took the large curry comb from the red metal grooming kit that belonged to Wildwood for all to use.

"You sure got dirty out there in the woods," Taylor remarked as she ran the brush down Prince Albert's flank, releasing a cloud of grime. "What were you doing? Why did you stay with that little fawn?"

Prince Albert sputtered, as if in reply. Taylor often felt that he was communicating with her either through the sounds he made or his expressive dark eyes. Sometimes she was even sure she knew what he was saying, but at other moments she wished they could talk more directly. Right then was one of those times.

Taylor wished Prince Albert could explain exactly why he'd stopped near the fawn and stayed there. Was he simply curious? Did he think he was protecting it? From what she'd seen, a horse would generally take off if it came upon a deer. Maybe the little fawn was so small and still that Prince Albert didn't understand what he was seeing. Was it possible he hadn't even noticed it there and had simply stopped by the creek to take a drink?

Glancing over her shoulder, she saw Mrs. LeFleur in the office sitting behind her big, worn-looking desk and talking to someone on the phone and writing as she spoke. Her expression was especially serious and it worried Taylor. Mrs. LeFleur sensed Taylor's eyes on her and looked up. She waved, but her warm smile still hadn't returned. Taylor waved back nervously and then returned to brushing down Prince Albert.

After another five minutes or so, while Taylor was brushing bits of twigs and leaves from Prince Albert's mane, Mrs. LeFleur emerged from the office. "Almost done?" she asked as she tacked a notice onto the board.

"Almost," Taylor confirmed. "Mrs. LeFleur, I just want to say again how sor —"

"Please don't, Taylor. You've apologized more than enough. We all make mistakes. Heaven knows I've made my share of them. Forget about it now."

"I can't, but thank you," Taylor replied. "How is Mrs. Gonzalez? Have you heard?"

"Her leg is broken and she's extremely mad," Mrs. LeFleur replied. "I'm hoping my insurance will cover the cost of her car and any medical expenses. If it does, maybe she won't sue the ranch. Right now, that's what she's threatening to do."

"What would happen if she did that?" Taylor asked, pausing in the middle of a brushstroke.

Mrs. LeFleur sighed deeply. "It would be the end of the ranch. I'd have to close down. My insurance payments are going to triple even if she doesn't sue."

A knot formed in the pit of Taylor's stomach. Close the ranch? It couldn't happen. It just couldn't. "I'm really sor —"

Mrs. LeFleur held up her hand. "Don't! It's been a long day, and I need a break from the topic. It will all work out."

"But you can't close Wildwood," Taylor insisted urgently.

"We'll have to hope for the best," Mrs. LeFleur said wearily.

Taylor wanted to ask if Mrs. Gonzalez had said anything about Mercedes not being allowed back at the ranch, but she decided against it. Maybe Mercedes had talked her mother out of it by now, and there was no point in worrying Mrs. LeFleur any further.

Taylor walked Prince Albert back to his stall and maneuvered him inside with gentle guidance. "I'm so glad you're safe," she said, laying her cheek on Prince Albert's sturdy neck. "I couldn't have stood it if anything had happened to you." Coming in front of him, she rubbed her forehead on his muzzle. "You're such a good boy, and I love you so much."

In the stall next door, Pixie neighed as if to ask, *What about me?* Looking at her, Taylor smiled. "And you're a good girl, too. You found Prince Albert today. Nice job."

Stroking Prince Albert's forelock, she remembered the sharp blast of gunfire ringing through the woods, and it made her shudder. What if Prince Albert had been hit as he ran freely among the trees? It was too awful to even think about.

A noise made Taylor turn to the back door nearest Prince Albert's stall. Someone was standing out in the rain. In the near darkness, Taylor couldn't make out who it was, but then Mercedes stepped inside, water dripping from her abundant, thick, dark curls.

"You're soaked!" Taylor said, locking Prince Albert into his stall and hurrying to her side. "Are you okay? How's your mother? How did you get here?"

Mercedes shivered as she folded her arms together for warmth. Her teeth were chattering so hard that Taylor could hear them clacking together. "We took a car service from the hospital, and Mom went right to bed. Once she was sleeping, I walked here."

Taylor pulled off her zipper-front sweatshirt and handed it to Mercedes. "Put this on."

Waving it away, Mercedes shook her head. "Then you'll be cold."

"I'm not dripping wet like you are," Taylor insisted, pressing the sweatshirt into Mercedes' arms.

Again Mercedes declined, handing the sweatshirt back to Taylor. "There's the horse sheet in the tack room. I'll wrap myself in that."

Taylor followed Mercedes up the center aisle to the tack room. Pulling the blue plaid sheet from a shelf, Mercedes shook it out, wrapping it around her shoulders. "That's better."

"How's your mother?" Taylor asked again.

"Terrible. Her leg hurts a lot, and she's taking it out on me, making my life terrible, too," Mercedes answered angrily. "I feel sorry for her, but she's being so awful that it isn't easy. She keeps shouting about the ranch and how it's all Wildwood's fault. Can you believe she doesn't want me coming back here? It's so stupid! It's not like

Mrs. LeFleur lets the horses wander around on the road. It was an accident!"

"It was *my* fault. I'm sorry."

"Don't be sorry. It *wasn't* your fault. Stupid Plum Mason's idiot mother made Prince Albert bolt. Daphne called to see how I was, and she told me the whole story."

They came out into the center aisle and stood in front of the bulletin board. Taylor noticed the flyer Mrs. LeFleur had put up and began to read it.

**SATURDAY, NOVEMBER 5**
**HORSE EVENT**
**SPONSORED BY**
**ROSS RIVER RANCH**

There was a list of events from advanced hunter–jumper competitions to endurance raising and dressage events. But the one that interested Taylor read:

**SPECIAL EVENT FOR BEGINNER JUMPERS**
**FIRST PRIZE:**
**FIVE FREE LESSONS AT ROSS RIVER RANCH**

Taylor turned to Mercedes. "Imagine getting lessons at Ross River," she said. Riding lessons at the fanciest, most expensive ranch in the whole area would be too awesome.

"Enter the contest," Mercedes suggested.

"I never learned how to jump, or even how to ride English style. There's no jumping in Western riding, which is all I know. Daphne offered to teach me, but she keeps booking more and more lessons, which is great, but it means she has less and less time."

"I'll teach you," Mercedes offered.

"You will?" Taylor asked, surprised.

Mercedes nodded. "I want to get over to Ross River. You'd have to take me with you to the show, okay? That's my price for lessons."

"Sure. Why do you want to go? Are you going to enter?"

"I don't want to compete right now. I used to compete a lot when we lived in Connecticut, but I'm not that into it anymore. I'd just rather ride and jump on my own. It's not why I want to go to Ross River Ranch."

"What's the reason, then?" Taylor asked.

"There's a white horse there I want to see."

Taylor's eyes lit excitedly. "Are you going to buy it?"

Mercedes looked away uncomfortably. "No."

"Then why do you want to see it?"

"Because I just do," Mercedes insisted, still not looking directly at Taylor. "Don't ask so many questions."

"Okay, sorry," Taylor said. This was so odd. Why wouldn't she tell Taylor anything? "Come on, tell me what's so special about this white horse," she pressed.

"Why are you so nosy?" Mercedes snapped.

"Why are you so secretive?" Taylor shot back. "I was just interested to know."

"It's *my* business, okay?" Mercedes came back at her, clearly agitated.

Taylor didn't want to upset one more person, so she let it drop. "Do you really think I could I learn to jump in time?" she asked.

"Sure you could," Mercedes said, seeming relieved that the subject had been changed. "It's not like you're a total beginner at riding."

A smile slowly formed on Taylor's face. Learning to ride English style and to jump had long been one of her goals. She loved to pore through catalogs of English riding gear and to admire the gorgeous outfits with their gleaming boots, crisp blazers, velvet helmets, and slim breeches.

"But wait!" Taylor said, her smile fading fast. "You're not allowed to come to the ranch anymore, are you?"

An expression of hard determination came to Mercedes' face. "She can't stop me."

"Ummm." Taylor hesitated. "I hate to say this but . . . she sort of can."

"How?" Mercedes demanded.

"She's your mother."

Mercedes shrugged. "So? She works in the city and isn't home till seven every night. How will she know?"

"Someone might tell her," Taylor suggested.

"Like who?"

"I don't know," Taylor admitted. "Anyone. You never know."

"She started this job in the city the first week we moved. She doesn't have a single friend here."

"But won't she be home now that her leg is broken?" Taylor questioned.

Mercedes considered this a moment before answering. "Maybe. For a few days. But she'll go back. She's pretty devoted to her job now that she's the only one . . ."

Taylor waited for her to finish the sentence. "The only one what?" she pressed gently after several more minutes.

"Nothing!" Mercedes said crisply. "Do you want me to teach you to jump or not?"

"Definitely! But I don't want you to get into trouble."

"I won't get into trouble," Mercedes insisted. "And besides, I don't care. When the thing happened with our horses, I lost them all. And then we had to move. Now I've found a way to have horses again, and she's not taking it away from me."

Taylor studied Mercedes a moment, deciding what to say to her. She didn't want to say the wrong thing and upset her even more. *Something* had happened to Mercedes' family that she never wanted to talk about. But maybe this was the time to get an answer since Mercedes had brought it up. "What happened?" Taylor asked cautiously.

Mercedes looked like she was about to reply but then turned away. "Nothing! Just tell me — yes or no — do you want me to teach you to ride English?"

"Yes," Taylor agreed. "Yes."

"Great," Mercedes said. "We can start next Saturday morning. How about at nine o'clock?"

"Okay. Nine," Taylor agreed. A smile grew on her face. She was going to learn to ride English style — at last!

# Chapter 9

Taylor sat in the passenger seat beside her mother, Jennifer, who had come to the ranch to pick her up. The winding roads were dark along here without sidewalks or streetlights. The rain pelted the car, dashed from view by the continual slapping of the wipers against the front windshield.

Mercedes was in the backseat and they were headed to drop her off at her house which, she said, was about a mile down the road from the ranch. Taylor had never been to Mercedes' house, and she was intensely curious to see what it looked like.

Taylor's mother was still in the white shirt and black pants she wore to her job at the Pheasant Valley Diner.

Taylor's parents had divorced back in the spring. Jennifer had started her own catering business, and it was beginning to do well, but not so well that Jennifer could quit her waitress job.

"So, you girls have had some day," Jennifer commented as she steered through the rainstorm after Taylor and Mercedes told her everything that had happened; everything except that Mercedes had been forbidden to return to the ranch. Without discussing it, the girls had both left that part out. It didn't seem wise to Taylor to let her mom know that Mercedes was supposed to be at home at the moment. Parents had a way of talking to one another.

Around the next bend, they entered a neighborhood where the houses were set back far from the road. "There it is. I can get off right here," Mercedes said, pointing to a modest split ranch home at the end of long driveway.

"I'll drive you to the door," Jennifer offered.

"No, no," Mercedes declined quickly. "Mom might still be sleeping, and I don't want to wake her."

Taylor and Mercedes exchanged quick glances over this lie. Mercedes had already told Taylor that her bedroom was on the first floor and she would have no trouble slipping back in, unnoticed, as if she'd never left.

"But it's pouring," Jennifer objected, turning into the driveway. "I can't let you walk all that way in the rain."

The house was dark, and Taylor hoped it would stay that way. If a light came on it would mean Mrs. Gonzalez was up. Mercedes and Taylor exchanged another tense look as the car neared the front of the house.

The car's headlights, two beams shot through with crystal raindrops, illuminated the driveway. Taylor peered ahead, trying to get a better look at the house. She knew that back when Mercedes lived in Connecticut she had owned a number of horses, which suggested that her family was wealthy. Through the rain and darkness, Taylor was able to see a rather plain house that was even a bit run-down looking.

The second the car stopped, Mercedes had her hand on the car door handle, eager to leave. "Thanks so much, Mrs. Henry. See you at our first lesson, Taylor. Bye."

"Turn on a light so I know you got in safely," Jennifer instructed.

"Okay," Mercedes agreed. In a second she was gone, disappearing into the darkness of her backyard. Taylor and her mother sat in silence until a bottom floor light snapped on. Then Taylor's mother backed down the driveway, her head craned toward the rear window. "Okay, what's going on?" she asked.

"Nothing. What do you mean?" Taylor replied, trying to sound as innocent as possible.

"Taylor," Jennifer prodded insistently.

Why did her mother have to be so difficult to fool all the time? Taylor's mind raced. Should she tell the truth or stick with her story?

"Mercedes is not supposed to come to Wildwood anymore," she admitted. "Her mother thinks it was careless the way I let Prince Albert get out into the road."

Jennifer Henry's right eyebrow arched. "She thinks it's *your* fault?" she questioned.

Taylor nodded.

"And that's what you two were covering up — that Mercedes wasn't supposed to be at Wildwood?"

"Yep."

"Where did her mother think Mercedes was?"

"I guess she's asleep and doesn't know Mercedes was out of the house." Taylor looked at her mother, trying hard to gauge her expression. She decided it could best be described as thoughtful, which didn't really help.

"Are you going to call Mrs. Gonzalez?" Taylor asked at last.

Her mother didn't reply at first, but the lost-in-thought expression remained on her face. "No," she finally answered decisively. "It's between Mercedes and her mother. I would only call if Mercedes was doing something dangerous or harmful."

Taylor slumped slightly with relief. Not only would this mean Mercedes wasn't in trouble, it also meant she could teach Taylor to ride English style.

They took the rest of the trip home in silence. Taylor gazed out the window as the car's headlights swept light through the rainy darkness.

Suddenly, Taylor gasped.

"What?" her mother asked.

"We just passed a dead deer off to the side of the road," Taylor reported.

"Oh, poor thing," Jennifer commented sympathetically.

It wasn't that uncommon to see dead deer in Pheasant Valley. They were overabundant and often ran recklessly into the road, startling drivers. Taylor had grown up seeing roadkill like this all her life.

But tonight she was thinking of the fawn hiding in the woods waiting for its mother. Was it still there waiting?

Taylor was about to turn off the bedroom light on her nightstand when her cell phone buzzed. When she saw it was Daphne, she clicked the call through right away.

"How are you feeling?" Daphne asked. "Is everything okay?"

"I'm totally zonked," Taylor admitted. "I'd be asleep already except I had homework. Thanks for all your help today."

"Sure." Daphne asked if Mrs. LeFleur had heard any more from Mrs. Gonzalez, and Taylor told her about the possibility of a lawsuit. "That would be horrible," Daphne said. "Maybe Mercedes can talk her mother out of it."

"Maybe," Taylor agreed, but she couldn't really imagine that happening. Mrs. Gonzalez didn't strike her as someone who could be easily influenced. She seemed very strong-minded.

Talking about Mercedes made Taylor remember to tell Daphne about the contest at Ross River Ranch and that Mercedes was going to teach her to ride English and jump.

"I was going to teach you!" Daphne objected.

"You're so busy, though," Taylor pointed out.

"I know. I'm sorry."

"When you used to board Mandy over at Ross River, do you remember seeing a white horse over there?" Taylor asked. "Mercedes is determined to get over there to look at some white horse, but she won't say why."

"She's always so secretive about everything," Daphne commented. "I wonder why."

"I know," Taylor agreed. "She got all annoyed with me when I asked her questions today. I saw her house when we dropped her off."

"Is she rich?" Daphne asked.

"Her house was nice, but it didn't look rich," Taylor reported. "Anyway, do you know anything about this white horse?"

"I know there's a beautiful white Missouri Fox Trotting gelding over there," Daphne recalled. "I think it came in this last spring when Mrs. Ross bought a bunch of horses at a great price from someone who was closing down their whole stable."

"What's that breed like?" Taylor asked.

"It's a little like Jojo, the Tennessee walking horse that Eric owns," Daphne said. "It's a great general, all-around horse. It's good for showing and covering long distances. Do you think Mercedes wants to buy it?"

"I asked her and she said no."

"Hmm, that's strange," Daphne remarked. "Did her mom say she could come back to the barn?"

"No, but she's determined to, anyway. She thinks her mom won't find out."

"She does, huh?" Daphne said. "What if her mom *does* find out and gets so mad that she definitely decides to sue Wildwood?"

"Mrs. LeFleur says she'd have to close the place down."

"Close down!" Daphne cried. "Are you sure?"

"That's what she said," Taylor confirmed, and found that her voice cracked with worry as she spoke the words.

"Oh, I almost forgot to tell you," Daphne said. "I think Mercedes has a crush on some guy named Monty. Do you know him? Do any customers named Monty come around Wildwood when I'm not there?"

Taylor thought. "No. . . . Does anyone in the high school have that name?"

"No. But I saw one of Mercedes' notebooks the other day, and she'd written the name Monty all over it. That girl sure has a lot of secrets!"

Taylor couldn't agree more.

# Chapter 10

"You're not going anywhere with stirrups *that* long," Mercedes said. It was the following Saturday morning, and Mercedes was standing in the middle of the oval paddock to the side of the main building across from the open stalls. Taylor and Prince Albert were inside the paddock, standing beside its split-rail fence.

Taylor stopped beside Prince Albert and looked quizzically at the hunt seat saddle she was placing on his back. She had called Daphne that morning and gotten her permission to borrow it. It was easy for Taylor to figure out how the saddle worked after years of looking through catalogs and magazines featuring

English riding outfits and gear. She was proud she had gotten it on correctly. Now what was Mercedes saying she'd done wrong?

"This isn't Western, remember?" Mercedes said. "English riders use a shorter stirrup so that they can post during the trot and go into two-point over jumps. Now shorten those up, and hop on," she commanded, crossing her arms.

Taylor felt a quick wrinkle of annoyance at Mercedes' bossy tone of voice, but she obeyed, not wanting to cause any tension during her first lesson. Mercedes was being nice enough to teach her, so it wasn't worth an argument. She knew how overbearing Mercedes could be, but the barn's assistant junior manager was also an excellent horsewoman, and Taylor would learn a lot from her. Besides, Mercedes didn't mean anything by it. Taking charge was simply part of the girl's personality, and Taylor was almost used to it.

Shortening the stirrups a few holes, she glanced at Mercedes for confirmation. Mercedes nodded impatiently from the middle of the ring, beckoning her to hurry. Taylor tightened the girth, pulling upward on the leather straps holding the elastic ends in.

This made sense to Taylor because she tightened Western saddles in this way, too. Prince Albert, like all horses, would "blow out." This meant he would push his muscles out when a rider tightened his girth, so that later on, when he relaxed his muscles, the girth would be looser. They called it blowing out because people thought horses were extending their stomachs, but in reality they were just tensing their muscles. Though it might feel good for the horses, it could be bad for the rider if his or her saddle slipped dangerously and caused a fall.

Taylor stuck her left foot into the stirrup, swinging her body up and over. The English saddle felt uncomfortably small and cramped underneath her. She grabbed the reins in her right hand and clucked Prince Albert forward at a walk.

"Uh . . . stop. One problem," Mercedes interrupted.

Taylor halted Prince Albert, staring questioningly at Mercedes.

"Your reins. You're trying to do neck reining, but English riders do split reining. That means one rein in each hand. Here," Mercedes instructed, striding over and fixing Taylor's hands. Taylor nodded, letting Mercedes mold her hands into the proper position.

"There. Now you're ready. Do a lap at the walk and get used to the tack. It'll feel a lot smaller than those big clunky Western saddles because, well, it is." Mercedes said.

Taylor did as instructed, trying to relax into the saddle. She took a deep breath, both nervous and excited to finally be one step closer to jumping. After a lap around the ring, Taylor was feeling slightly more at ease.

"All right. Comfy? Now, pick up your trot," Mercedes called to Taylor.

"Is that the same thing as the jog?" Taylor shouted back, not completely confident about how the Western terms translated to the English jargon.

"Yeah, sort of. Just a little faster," Mercedes replied. "Almost everything in English is faster than Western. That's why all English riders have to use helmets, even though higher level Western riders can just wear cowboy hats in competitions," Mercedes explained.

She was bossy, but she sure knew her stuff.

Taylor picked up the jog and then urged Prince Albert into a trot. She bounced around in the saddle, trying to sit still, but finding it tougher at this quicker pace.

"Post!" shouted Mercedes. Taylor stared at her, trying to focus on the bouncing image of Mercedes.

"What? What's post?" Taylor shouted back.

"Posting is when you rise up and down out of the saddle with the rhythm of the horse at the trot. It'll make the trot way less bouncy."

Taylor tightened her abdominal and thigh muscles in her attempt to lift in the saddle. It wasn't easy, but the ride did become much more controlled and was certainly not as hard on her butt.

"Don't mess up your diagonals!" Mercedes commanded.

Taylor stopped Prince Albert and stared at Mercedes.

Split reins?

Posting?

Diagonals?

There were so many terms to learn! Taylor took a deep breath, trying to remain calm but getting increasingly frustrated. Noticing Taylor's expression, Mercedes chuckled softly, walking over to Prince Albert again.

"I'm sorry, Taylor. I forget you're completely new to hunt seat," she said in a surprisingly comforting tone. "You seem so confident at Western that I just sort of assume you know stuff about English, too."

A soft smile spread across Taylor's lips. Did she really

just get a compliment from Mercedes? She took another deep breath and nodded. "Well, thanks. Yeah, it's a lot to learn, but I think I'll get it," Taylor responded, feeling slightly refreshed by Mercedes' compliment.

"You will. Okay, so, a diagonal is when the horse's outside front leg goes forward — that's the signal to the rider to rise out of the saddle. It's an easy rhythm once you get it," she explained, moving back into the center of the ring to watch Taylor. "Try it!

"Up, down, up, down, up . . ." Mercedes counted in rhythm as Taylor attempted to post. Taylor urged Prince Albert forward into a trot, which he picked up right away, ears perked. She pushed down into her heels, trying to push her bottom out of the saddle in time with the horse.

After doing this for a quarter of a lap, Taylor glanced over at Mercedes for a reaction.

Mercedes was watching, pursing her lips. She didn't seem entirely satisfied by what she was seeing.

Taylor's heart pounded as sweat formed on her brow. This was so much more work than Western style! She concentrated on trying to keep the rhythm, which was proving more difficult than she had expected.

"You're on the wrong diagonal!" Mercedes shouted from the center. Taylor glanced down as Prince Albert's outside leg swung forward. *Darn*, Taylor thought.

"Sit two beats and you'll be on the right diagonal again," Mercedes explained, hands on her hips.

Taylor sat, counting "One, two," and tried to rise back up in rhythm.

"Still wrong," Mercedes grumbled, rubbing her temple.

Taylor sighed. *This better be worth it in the long run*, she thought to herself.

# Chapter 11

After her lesson, Taylor helped Mercedes muck and hay the stalls, then water and feed all the horses, even though it wasn't her day to do those chores. It was the least she could after Mercedes had spent so much time teaching her to ride English.

"So, how's your mother?" Taylor asked as she raked out the old hay in Shafir's empty stall.

Mercedes was loading new hay into Pixie's stall while the little pony stood in the center aisle, watching. "The same and crankier than ever; she went to her orthopedist in New Jersey today so I was able to get away. She's going back to work on Monday, so that part is great."

"Do you think she'll sue the ranch?" Taylor asked, voicing the question that had been in the back of her mind all day.

Mercedes stopped raking. "If she does, I'll never speak to her again."

Taylor looked at Mercedes. From the determined set of the girl's jaw, she felt certain that Mercedes meant what she'd said. It didn't seem useful to point out that it would be pretty difficult for Mercedes to never speak to her mother, so Taylor just nodded. "I'd probably feel the same way if I were you," she remarked sympathetically.

"She'd better not do it," Mercedes said, throwing herself into laying down Pixie's hay with extra energy.

A mischievous impulse seized Taylor, and she couldn't resist it. "So tell me about Monty," she said.

Mercedes stood straight and stared at Taylor, her face going pale. "Who told you about Monty?" she demanded harshly.

It wasn't the reaction Taylor had expected, and she was suddenly sorry she'd brought it up. "Monty," she repeated weakly. "Isn't he a guy you like?"

Dropping her hunched shoulders, Mercedes appeared

to relax a little. "Yeah, Monty. He's just a guy at school. You must have seen his name on my notebook, huh?"

Taylor remembered Daphne saying there was no one at the high school named Monty, and Daphne knew just about everyone. Taylor decided not to press it. She already felt like she'd pried too much into Mercedes' privacy. "Yeah, that's why I asked," she said.

"Just some guy I used to like. I don't even think about him anymore," Mercedes said, returning to laying down hay.

When they were done, Mercedes rushed off, eager to get home before her mother returned from the bone doctor. Taylor watched her hurry away and sighed, turning to Prince Albert in his stall. "Do you get the feeling that she might not be as tough as she sometimes seems?" she asked him.

It was a hunch, a feeling that maybe Mercedes had been through a lot, and she also had a mother who wasn't easy to deal with. Taylor realized that she felt sympathy and a feeling of friendship toward Mercedes that hadn't been there before today. "She's really okay," Taylor told Prince Albert, "once you get to know her."

By six o'clock that Saturday, Taylor was in the stable's wide main aisle, brushing down Prince Albert's sweat-damp black coat. Prince Albert's harness was hooked onto the rings just outside the front office.

Prince Albert sputtered and Taylor smiled. She knew Prince Albert loved her as much as she loved him. Taylor couldn't imagine ever loving another horse as much as she loved Prince Albert.

From her position on Prince Albert's right side, Taylor could see Mrs. LeFleur inside the office, talking on the phone. Outside, by the last of the day's dying light, Plum worked Shafir in the front main paddock. She'd been out there since one that afternoon. Taylor stopped brushing and watched Plum as she cantered in a circle and then jumped Shafir over a low crossbar that she'd set up, doing it again and again.

*Plum works that horse way too hard*, Taylor thought, and was instantly struck with a pang of guilt. At one time, Plum and her mother had considered leasing Prince Albert, but Taylor had worked hard to make sure that didn't happen. Two previous horses that Plum had leased died under her rough riding and lack of proper aftercare and grooming. It was Taylor who had steered Plum toward leasing Shafir instead.

When Mrs. Ross had donated her, Shafir was nearly wild and refused to be ridden. Daphne and Mercedes had put in a lot of work to settle and train Shafir so Wildwood could use her. They also did it so Plum wouldn't. They saw how rough Plum was with Shafir and didn't want the horse damaged. Taylor had learned a lot by helping Daphne and Mercedes in the training process.

Mrs. LeFleur came out of the office. "How did your first English lesson go?" she inquired.

"My whole body hurts," Taylor admitted. "That posting stuff kills my legs."

Mrs. LeFleur grinned. "It can be rough at first," she said. "Do they feel like rubber bands?"

"Yes!" Taylor replied. "Sore rubber bands!"

"You'll get used to it," Mrs. LeFleur assured her. "Where did this sudden urge to learn English style come from?"

"It's something I've wanted to learn for a long time," Taylor said as she pointed to the notice on the bulletin board. "But now I need to learn fast, because I want to win the five free lessons at Ross River."

"You're going to learn to jump by November fifth?" Mrs. LeFleur asked. "Don't you think that's a bit soon?"

Taylor tilted her head toward Plum. "If she can do it, I can."

"Plum's had a lot of experience and lots of lessons," Mrs. LeFleur pointed out.

"That's exactly what I need, too," Taylor insisted. "More lessons."

"But I thought Daphne was going to help you with that."

"She's really busy with her paying customers and school and all. I've heard that Ross River has great instructors."

"Of course they do. Everyone over there is rich," Mrs. LeFleur reminded Taylor, her voice tinged with annoyance. "You can have great everything when you're rich."

"I'd sure have great everything if *I* were rich," Taylor said, returning her brush to the grooming kit and taking out the hoof pick to clean Prince Albert's shoes. "What's wrong with that?"

"Oh, nothing's wrong with it," Mrs. LeFleur allowed. "I just wonder how much those people over there appreciate their horses. A lot don't even groom them."

"Don't you have to groom your horse?" Taylor asked, bending over Prince Albert's back hoof as she worked to remove debris.

"No. Barn hands do it for them a lot of the time."

Taylor knew she wouldn't have liked that. The time she spent grooming Prince Albert — and Pixie, too — made her happy. She liked cleaning them till they glistened and tucking them into their stalls for the night, smelling good and ready to rest.

Looking out to the paddock, Taylor saw Plum sail over the jump. "They've been doing that since one o'clock," she said to Mrs. LeFleur. "Do you think that's too much?"

"Possibly," Mrs. LeFleur agreed. "And it's almost dark." Pulling her barn jacket tighter against the late afternoon chill, Wildwood's owner headed out to talk to Plum.

Taylor could see Plum arguing with Mrs. LeFleur, but finally she gave in and turned Shafir toward the paddock gate. Mrs. LeFleur returned to the main building and went into the office, followed by Plum on Shafir at a walk.

Not wanting to stare, Taylor busied herself with Prince Albert's hooves. She noticed that his right back shoe seemed just a little loose; not too bad, but just the same, Taylor made a mental note to mention it to Norman the farrier when he came to the barn on his monthly visit.

When she glanced up again, Plum was about to dismount just outside the stable's entrance. "Aren't you going to cool her down?" Taylor objected. "She's got to be way overheated after all that jumping."

Plum sat back in her saddle and glared at Taylor. "What's it to you?" she challenged.

Red fury shot up into Taylor's face. What was it to her? How could she ask that? Shafir was a gorgeous, playful, young horse! Anyone would care that she be cooled down and groomed properly — anyone, of course, but Plum.

She bit back on her angry words. Things were bad enough between Plum and Taylor after what had happened with Prince Albert. For the sake of Wildwood she didn't want to make them worse. "I'll cool her down if you want," Taylor offered.

Plum swung her leg around and dropped from the saddle. "Do what you like. But she might not let you ride her."

Even though Shafir was leased from Wildwood, Plum acted as though she owned the mare and that they had a close relationship. Taylor had never seen any indication of that, though. "Oh, I've ridden her before," Taylor replied casually.

It wasn't true. Daphne and Mercedes were training Shafir in the English style. Although Taylor had helped them, she'd never actually ridden the chestnut Arabian. She just couldn't bring herself to give Plum the satisfaction of knowing that.

"Really? You've ridden her?" Plum remarked coldly. "I'm surprised."

Fearing that her face would give away the lie, Taylor ducked it down as she unclipped Prince Albert's harness from the rings.

Holding the harness's side strap, she walked Prince Albert to his stall at the far end of the stable. Pixie neighed in greeting from her adjoining stall. "Your friend is back," Taylor said, smiling at the pony.

Cody glanced curiously out of his stall and neighed.

"I'll be back to give you guys fresh water before I leave," Taylor assured them. "And if you're good, I'll give you a horse treat from the front office."

When Taylor returned, Plum was gone. If her mother had come to pick her up, Taylor was glad they'd missed each other. Since Plum had left her unhitched and unattended, Shafir had wandered toward the back pasture, her reins dragging. Jogging toward her, Taylor caught up with the Arabian and picked up her reins. She put her boot in the stirrup and swung into the saddle. "Let's take a walk, pretty girl," she cooed to the horse. "You've had a hard day."

Shafir was much smaller and more fine-boned than Prince Albert. Taylor was glad now that the English saddle wasn't as strange to her as it had felt earlier when she first encountered it.

With a gentle click, Taylor headed Shafir up to the pasture between the woods and the barn, stroking her silky chestnut neck as they walked. When they got to the pasture's fence, Taylor took the opportunity to work on the new skill Daphne was teaching her — to open a gate without dismounting. It was mostly a matter of staying balanced in the saddle as she reached over and down to lift the latch.

When Taylor had opened the gate, ridden through, and resecured the lock, she felt proud of her accomplishment. Her skills as a horsewoman had improved greatly from being at Wildwood and learning from Mercedes and especially Daphne. So much had happened since Mrs. LeFleur had reopened the ranch, and mostly it had all been good — very, very good. In Taylor's view, Wildwood was the best place in the entire world.

Taylor meandered around the field at a walk, her path lit by the full moon, which illuminated the grasses and leaves so that they seemed to gleam on their own power. The two outside lights down at the stable turned on. It was later than Taylor had realized. Mrs. LeFleur would want to be going soon, and she was giving Taylor a ride home. She still had to give Shafir a quick grooming before they could leave. "I hope you're cooled down enough, because we have to go back," she told the mare as she turned her back toward the gate.

Shafir suddenly stopped and her ears flattened. Swishing her tail, she threw back her head and neighed shrilly.

Taylor sat tall in her saddle, all her senses alert. What had bothered Shafir so much?

And then she heard it.

Off in the distance . . . the howl of coyotes. And the first picture that flashed into Taylor's head was of the small fawn, waiting for its mother in the high grass.

# Chapter 12

That night Taylor came home to find Claire sitting at the kitchen table beside her mother. Both of them were making carrot curls over large wooden bowls of salad. Claire often helped Jennifer with her new catering business. "Hey, Taylor, you're home late," her mother's friend commented.

"Yeah, I expected you a half hour ago," Jennifer added, with a touch of annoyance. "We've talked about this, and I've said —"

"I texted you," Taylor interrupted. Taking a seat beside Claire, she petted Bunny, Claire's brindle-coated pit bull, who arose from her sleeping place under the table to greet her.

"I didn't get it," Jennifer protested.

"Look at your phone," Taylor insisted.

Jennifer reached into the pocket of her jeans and pulled out her cell phone. "Oh," she said sheepishly.

"You can't keep it on silent all the time," Taylor scolded mildly.

"I did a luncheon for a church group today and didn't want it to ring while the minister was speaking," Jennifer explained. "I must have forgotten to turn it back on." She read the message, which Taylor knew said HOME A LTTLE LTR. STILL @ BARN COOLNG SHAFIR.

"You have to keep up with the cell phone, Jen," Claire teased her friend.

"Oh, give me a break," Jennifer mumbled, stretching cellophane wrap over one of the bowls. "I just forgot to turn on the ring tone."

"If you're going to do that, check for messages once in a while," Claire insisted.

Taylor looked down at Bunny, hiding her smile. She loved the way Claire gently teased her mom. They'd known each other since grade school, and there was nothing they couldn't say to each other. Taylor wondered if she and Travis would have that kind of friendship when they were older. She hoped so.

Looking up again, Taylor met Claire's eyes. "Do you remember the fawn we found in the woods?" she asked.

"Uh-huh."

"Do you have any time to go with me and check on it?"

"I'm sure it's long gone by now," Claire said.

Jennifer tore more cellophane wrap from the roll. "Why do you want to look for it, Taylor?" she asked.

"I'm just worried," Taylor replied. "We saw that dead female deer on the road last night, and this evening I heard coyotes howling."

Claire frowned. "I heard them, too, a couple of nights ago. Some of my feral cats are missing." Claire tended to the homeless cats in the neighborhood — as well as a wide assortment of other animals — and had a two-story shed for them. "The ferals roam pretty far into the woods at night, and I wonder if a coyote got them. Something got into my neighbor's chicken coop, too. Could have been raccoons, but there was a print in the chicken yard that was definitely canine."

"I just want to take a look. Could we?" Taylor asked.

"If the mother really hasn't come back it might be too late already," Claire said. "I'm just warning you."

Taylor and Claire had run into some gruesome scenes

when they had gone out on animal rescues but arrived too late to save an animal caught in a trap or hit by a vehicle. "I know," she said. "But maybe we'll get there in time."

"Okay, kiddo. We can go take a look tomorrow morning at nine if you like."

Taylor smiled at Claire. "Thanks."

"If it's still there, we just have to hope it survives the night," Claire said.

Taylor glanced out the kitchen window at the fat, full, orange moon hovering above the black line of trees. Although all she could hear was a storm kicking up, she imagined she was listening to the coyotes' frightening howls mixed into the wind's blustery song.

"It's just down this way," Taylor said to Claire on Sunday morning as they hiked into the woods, wearing orange vests so hunters could easily see them. Hurrying behind Taylor, Claire carried a red woolen blanket bundled in her arms and a black knapsack filled with supplies slung over her shoulder.

Now and then a breeze would shower them with cold water from the leaves overhead. The storm that had blown through during the night had left everything wet and the path strewn with fallen autumn leaves.

Taylor ran ahead, hardly able to control herself from breaking into a run. "Here by the creek," she said to Claire.

"Calm yourself, Taylor," Claire said. "The chance of the fawn still being there is very slim. We're just going to check."

"That's right," Taylor agreed. "We should hope it's *not* there, because that will mean its mother came back for it."

"Exactly."

"That's all I want to know," Taylor said, "that it's okay." Part of her wanted to see the little spotted fawn again, but Taylor knew she should be hoping she didn't.

When Taylor reached the place where the creek ran, she could hardly contain her excitement. From the path, she could see the clump of tall grass but couldn't tell if the fawn was there.

"Let me go first," Claire said, getting ahead of Taylor as she descended the slope going to the creek. She didn't say "Just in case we find something awful," but Taylor knew it was what Claire was thinking.

Staying close behind Claire, Taylor followed her across the creek, hopping from rock to rock to get to the far side.

Slowly, they approached the grassy patch where the fawn had been hiding.

Taylor's breath caught in her throat. There was something in the grass. She clutched at the sleeve of Claire's woolen jacket.

"I see," Claire whispered in response. She put her right index finger to her lip. "We don't want to scare it," she murmured.

The tiny fawn slept, its head down, its spindly legs sprawled around it. Its shallow breath rose and fell.

"Its mother hasn't come back, or she would have moved it," Claire said quietly, squatting down beside it. "It must be starving."

Without opening its eyes, the fawn stuck out its tongue and lapped up drops of rain still clinging to nearby blades of grass. At least it was getting some water.

Taylor knelt beside Claire just as the fawn slowly opened its brown eyes. Frightened, it tried to stand, but its sticklike legs buckled, and it couldn't get up. Claire placed her hand on the frightened animal. "Get me the bottle from my backpack," she told Taylor.

Moving fast as she could, Taylor found the bottle and took it from Claire's pack. "What's in it?" she asked as she handed it to Claire.

"It's a kind of baby formula for fawns. I contacted people who do deer rescue last night, and this is what they told me to give it."

The little deer sucked eagerly at the bottle as soon as Claire presented it. It bleated for more.

"Oh, my gosh! It sounds like a little lamb!" Taylor exclaimed. She'd always thought deer were completely silent.

Despite the fawn's pleading, Claire withdrew the bottle. "That's enough for now," she cooed to the fawn. "You haven't eaten in a few days. We don't want you to get sick."

"What do we do now?" Taylor asked.

"We're taking it," Claire replied. She bundled the blanket around the fawn and lifted it. "Scoot the blanket underneath," she instructed Taylor.

Together, they managed to bundle the baby into Claire's arms. "It's not as heavy as I would have thought," Claire commented.

"Will it be okay?" Taylor asked anxiously.

"It doesn't look injured," Claire remarked, looking the animal up and down. "No coyote or anything seems to have bothered it."

Taylor sighed with relief. "That's great."

Claire waded into the creek, still holding the deer. "I can't take the chance of dropping it while I hop the rocks," she explained.

Taylor admired Claire's toughness. The creek's rushing water had to be ice-cold, but Claire kept slogging through it, holding the fawn tightly.

"What will we do with it?" Taylor asked when Claire and the deer were out of the creek.

"I'm not sure," Claire admitted. "There are places that do deer rehab. I'll get in touch with them."

Off in the distance, a rifle sounded.

"Come on, let's get back to Wildwood," Claire suggested, heading for the path.

When they arrived back at the main building, Mrs. LeFleur was just pulling in. "Oh, my good heavens!" she cried when she saw the fawn. "What a beautiful little creature."

"Can I make it a bed in one of your empty stalls?" Claire requested.

"As long as I don't have a horse to board in there, yes, I suppose so," Mrs. LeFleur agreed.

"Should I get some hay?" Taylor asked.

"Good idea," Claire said.

In a short while they had built up a mound of hay and laid the baby deer, still wrapped in its blanket, inside it. "That should keep it nice and warm," Claire said.

"Can I feed it some more?" Taylor asked.

"A little more," Claire agreed, taking the bottle from her pack and handing it to Taylor. "Sit down in the hay, and I'll hand the fawn to you. It will probably be comforted by your heartbeat and your body warmth."

Taylor sat in the hay with her back to the wall, and Claire loaded the fawn into her lap. "Oh, it's so precious," Taylor whispered, overcome with fondness for the defenseless baby animal. Taking the bottle from Claire, she tipped it to the fawn's lips, and the baby guzzled voraciously.

"Not too much," Claire warned. "A little at a time."

Mrs. LeFleur came to watch alongside Claire. "It's good you went to look for it," she commented. "How did you know it would be there?"

"Taylor got worried when she saw a dead deer on the road and then heard coyotes at night," Claire told her.

"Yes, the coyotes worry me, too," Mrs. LeFleur agreed. "What if one got into the stable? I imagine in nature the horses would kick and rear. But in their stalls they're too confined to really defend themselves."

"Some people keep llamas," Claire said.

"Llamas?" Mrs. LeFleur echoed in surprise.

"Yeah," Claire said. "They're very fierce against coyotes, I hear."

Taylor was barely listening; all her attention was focused on the fawn. How sweet it was! It had waited so bravely for its mother to return, never wandering from its spot.

Mrs. LeFleur and Claire left her there with the fawn. Taylor fed it for a few more minutes, keeping her eyes on its lovely little face with its glistening black nose. Sensing that someone had come into the stall, Taylor glanced up and found Eric looking down at her.

"Hi, what are you doing here?" she asked quietly.

"I wanted to talk to Mrs. LeFleur," he said, coming inside and sitting on the floor beside her. "You look very natural sitting there feeding that fawn; like you've been doing it all your life."

Taylor smiled at that. "Thanks," she said. "But believe me, this is the first deer I have ever fed from a bottle."

"You'd never know it."

"What did you have to talk to Mrs. LeFleur about?" Taylor asked, pulling the bottle away as the fawn drifted to sleep in her arms.

"Remember I told you Ralph Westheimer laid me off?" Eric said, and Taylor nodded. "So I was wondering if Mrs. LeFleur could hire me."

"I doubt it. Her money is pretty tight. You know how we all volunteer here. And Mercedes has still been coming to the barn, even though she's not supposed to."

"Does Mrs. LeFleur know Mercedes isn't supposed to be coming here?" Eric asked.

"No," Taylor replied, shaking her head.

"Don't you think she should? Mercedes' mother might get even more angry at Wildwood if she finds out Mercedes has been coming to the ranch without permission."

"Maybe so," Taylor allowed, "but I don't want to be the one to tell her. You shouldn't, either."

Eric sighed. "If I volunteered to work for Jojo's board, do you think Mrs. LeFleur might go for *that*?"

"Possibly," Taylor considered. "That's how I board Pixie and Prince Albert here."

The fawn stirred in its sleep and then lifted its head, seeming to search for the bottle. "Want to feed it?" Taylor offered.

"Okay," Eric agreed, taking the bottle and holding it for the baby deer.

"Have you named it yet?" Eric asked softly.

"No. Do you think we should?" Taylor asked him. "We don't even know if it's a boy or a girl."

"Give it a name that would suit either way," Eric suggested.

Taylor gazed down at the white spots speckling the deer's soft brown coat. "Spots?" she suggested uncertainly. "Maybe not. It won't always have spots. A deer loses them as it gets older."

He nodded and stroked the fawn. "It must have been a late season birth, because a fawn is usually losing its spots by October. It's unusual, but I've seen spotted fawns in October occasionally."

Taylor looked at him with admiration. He seemed to know so many things in so many areas.

"I like the name Spots," Eric went on. "Later on, when the spots are gone, it will remind us of when it did have spots."

Taylor looked at Eric, and he met her gaze. Us? Taylor liked the sound of it. *Us.* She suddenly noticed that, for the first time, she felt comfortable with him, not all jumpy and nervous inside. It was a good feeling. "I suppose Spots could be an all right name," she agreed.

Taylor loved having Eric so close, right there next to her as she fed the deer. She felt so peaceful and happy. It seemed like one of those things that could only happen at Wildwood Stables.

# Chapter 13

By the following Saturday, Mercedes had given Taylor five more English riding lessons. Today, Taylor's legs ached from all the hard work as she stuck one foot in the stirrup and swung onto the saddle. She groaned, shifting around in the seat, fixing her stirrups to the appropriate shorter length.

"Come on! You can't be *that* tired, we haven't even started the good stuff yet!" Mercedes said, shaking her head.

Mercedes made her way over to the side of the corral and dragged out the PVC pipes they had been working on. Going over ground poles in two-point position was the intro to jumping. Taylor had been practicing her jumping position as Prince Albert trotted over the poles, picking up his knees so not to knock into them.

It helped that Prince Albert had clearly done all this before. At least one of them wasn't completely new to English riding. Mercedes had explained all the basics of jumping to Taylor and even lent her a book on it. All of it made sense to Taylor — but the thought of actually doing a jump made her stomach tighten with fear.

As Taylor began her warm-up laps at a walk, she noticed something different about today. Mercedes was dragging more poles than usual into the center of the ring. What was she planning?

After a few laps, Taylor picked up her trot, making certain to get the correct diagonal, just as Mercedes had taught her. She glanced down to Prince Albert's outside leg as it swung forward, while she rose out of the saddle at the same time. Mercedes had been right — English was a lot harder at first, but she had quickly gotten used to it.

"What're you using those extra poles for?" Taylor shouted to Mercedes, who was dragging what looked like even more pieces of jumps into the ring.

"I thought you said you wanted to learn how to jump," Mercedes responded, not turning to look at Taylor as she hoisted one of the pipes onto a rail. "I'm setting up cross rails for your first jump."

Taylor halted Prince Albert.

*Jump?*

*Now?*

It felt like she had only just begun to ride English!

Taylor's heart fluttered. She had been waiting for this for so long, and now that it was finally here, she was suddenly nervous. "But . . . uh . . . don't you think I should practice the poles some more?" she stammered, her voice suddenly small.

"Don't freak out on me. We've gotten this far, you're not backing down now," Mercedes demanded, folding her arms over her chest.

"But . . ." Taylor began to protest.

"No buts!" Mercedes insisted. "It's not even a big jump. It's the lowest the cross rail will go. You'll be fine."

"But, no," Taylor protested again. "I'm not ready."

"Taylor!" Mercedes shouted, throwing her arms wide with exasperation. "You have less than two more weeks until the competition! Did you forget that? I know it's a beginner's contest, but you have to *begin* to be a beginner."

Taylor cringed. She had just assumed that by the time Mercedes set up an actual jump she would feel ready. But she wasn't one bit ready!

"Just stay in your two-point when you go over," Mercedes told her, repeating instructions she'd already given to Taylor. "Give Prince Albert plenty of reins so he can stretch his neck out, and be strong. We've gone over this plenty of times. Now go! Try it!" Mercedes finished, looking at Taylor expectantly.

Taylor looked at the cross rail. It was two horizontal crossed pipes with a vertical supporting pipe at each end.

That was the lowest it would go?

It looked awfully high from Prince Albert's back.

Taylor took a deep breath and patted Prince Albert's neck, whispering to him. "You'll take care of me, boy, won't you?"

As he always did when she spoke to him, Prince Albert responded. This time it was with a neigh that Taylor wanted to believe sounded confident.

Taylor stroked his neck and sat upright. "Okay, let's try this jump!"

In the center of the ring, Mercedes tapped her foot,

clearly becoming impatient with Taylor's nervousness. Taking another deep breath, Taylor clucked at Prince Albert and trotted around the outside of the ring, keeping her eyes on the jump as Mercedes had told her to do.

She stared down at the jump as it got closer and closer.

Her grip on the reins tightened as they approached, and she leaned forward into her practiced two-point.

Taylor squeezed her eyes shut and winced as Prince Albert picked up his front two feet and hopped over the jump, clearing it with ease and landing lightly on the other side.

Mercedes laughed from the center of the ring as Taylor and Prince Albert trotted out of the jump.

"Don't shut your eyes next time!" she said, still laughing at Taylor's beginner mistake.

Taylor opened her eyes and looked around.

She had done it! Cleared her first jump! It was a bit jerkier than she had expected, but not that bad!

Her heart raced and adrenaline pumped through her system. Prince Albert even seemed to enjoy it as he pranced around the outside of the ring, ears perked, ready to go again.

"I did it! Prince Albert did it! We both did it!" Taylor shouted exuberantly, patting Prince Albert's neck.

"Now do it again — less sloppy this time, and with your eyes open!" Mercedes instructed.

"Sloppy?" Taylor frowned. She'd thought it had gone pretty well.

"Yes, sloppy. You were all hunched forward and crunching your face, like something was going to hit you," Mercedes told her. "Plus, your leg was way too far behind you. Pull that leg underneath your body, and I want you to sit up nice and straight, shoulders back, chin up, and look where you're going."

Taylor supposed Mercedes had a point. She *was* scared the first time, and her eyes *were* shut.

Nudging Prince Albert forward into a trot again, Taylor rounded the arena toward the jump. This time, she had her eyes glued on the cross rails. She made sure her leg was in the correct position, her shoulders were back, and her chin was up in an almost defiant manner.

Taking a deep breath as Prince Albert sped up a bit, she jumped. Grinning, Taylor watched the jump go by underneath her.

She'd cleared it!

That was perfect!

Mercedes couldn't say anything about that one!

Filled with pride, Taylor turned toward Mercedes. "How'd you like that?" she asked with a hint of boastfulness.

"Are you kidding?" Mercedes cried, slapping her palm to her forehead. "When I say 'keep your eyes on the jump' I don't mean stare at it like it's going to bite you!"

"I didn't!" Taylor protested.

"Always look where you *want* to go — not at the ground."

Taylor pouted for a lap. She thought she had done a good job on that one.

"Now, do it again," Mercedes demanded. "*Look* at the jump — don't bug-eyed *stare* at it. And make sure to breathe. You keep tensing up before going over. Jumping is supposed to be a very fluid motion, and you look so stiff up there."

"One more time. Okay, boy?" Taylor requested of Prince Albert, petting his neck again.

Prince Albert snorted and picked up his trot without even being asked. Taylor gritted her teeth in determination. She was going to make sure Mercedes had nothing bad to say about this next jump. She glanced down at Prince Albert's outside leg, rising up on the correct diagonal. She posted her way around the ring and was about to focus her gaze on the jump when someone standing at the gate caught her eye. She had a sinking feeling in her stomach. *Oh, no*, Taylor thought, *anyone but him*.

Prince Albert rounded the ring, heading toward the jump.

Eric was right there!

Watching!

Taylor's eyes instantly went from being fixed on the jump to being fixed on Eric.

"Pay attention!" Mercedes shouted, seeing Taylor's distraction.

But it was too late.

Prince Albert was already leaving the ground for the jump before Taylor could get up into position. Her breath caught in her throat as she was thrust backward.

Prince Albert sailed through the air — without her.

Taylor landed with a thud on her butt, dust flying up around her.

After clearing the jump, Prince Albert stopped on the other side. He turned around to look for his rider.

Taylor groaned and rubbed her back.

"Are you all right?" Eric shouted, hurrying forward from the gate to help her. He reached out a hand to her to pull her up.

Taylor's face flushed red with embarrassment. The hurt of being seen falling by Eric was much worse than the hurt of the actual fall. Prince Albert nickered loudly, as if to say, "Hey! You belong on my back, not on the ground!"

"Yeah, I'm fine. Thanks," Taylor grumbled, brushing the dirt off of her jeans. She didn't dare to make eye contact with Eric.

She'd fallen once before when he was around, but somehow this time it seemed more humiliating. Back then, she hadn't really known him too well. Now she could sense some new relationship was forming between them, and it was more important that he thought well of her.

Mercedes jogged forward, grabbing Prince Albert's reins.

"If you look at the ground, then that's where you're going to go!" Mercedes scolded, not at all concerned that Taylor had fallen.

Eric brushed some dirt off of Taylor's back. In another situation, she might have been thrilled to have him touching her, but this wasn't what she'd had in mind. "It's okay, everyone falls," he said kindly.

"That's what Daphne says," Taylor mentioned as she brushed dirt from her jeans.

"Because it's true," Eric said.

He was so sweet, and she liked him so much!

"Yeah, well, if she had been looking above the cross rails and not under them, she wouldn't have fallen," Mercedes put in.

"She's just learning," Eric defended Taylor.

"Did you talk to Mrs. LeFleur? Are you volunteering here now?" Taylor asked Eric hopefully, more than ready to change the subject.

"Yep."

"Great! And are you bringing JoJo here?"

"Uh-huh."

"Awesome! Is that why you're here today?"

"No, not really. Plum asked me to help her with her jumps. She's entering the beginner jumping contest over at Ross River."

Taylor stared at him, not sure of what she was hearing. "She's entering the advanced jumper, you mean." She was confident it was what he'd meant to say.

"No, the beginner," Eric insisted.

"Plum?!" Mercedes asked.

"But she's not a beginner," Taylor protested, her voice overlapping Mercedes'.

"She's not all that advanced, either. She's probably somewhere in between."

Taylor looked to Mercedes. "Can she do that?"

"I suppose it's up to her to decide what class she wants to be in," Mercedes replied. "Why is she doing it, though?"

"She wants the lessons," Eric answered. "They have great instructors over at Ross River."

"She wants to keep me from winning," Taylor argued, folding her arms angrily. "Are you helping her?" she asked Eric.

"She's my cousin," he answered.

Taylor didn't consider that a good enough answer, and she kept her angry gaze on Eric, silently waiting for more explanation.

"Okay, I *was* helping her because she's my cousin, but she was being such a little brat that I walked away and came over here," Eric admitted.

"You were going to help her beat me?" Taylor asked.

"What do you mean?"

"*I'm* entering that contest!"

"But this is your first jumping lesson, and the contest is less than two weeks away," Eric pointed out. "How can you possibly enter?"

"It's for *beginner* jumpers," Taylor reminded him.

"But you're not a beginner jumper. You're not even a jumper at all yet," Eric insisted.

"She will be!" Mercedes told Eric forcefully.

Eric quirked his mouth into a doubtful expression. "In two weeks?" he questioned.

Taylor started to speak, but Mercedes jumped in first. "*Yes!* In two weeks! I've taught other riders to jump in two weeks. Taylor is not exactly a beginning *rider.*"

"Don't get mad," Eric said, holding his palms up to them. "I just didn't think you would enter a contest like that because you ride Western. So I didn't see any harm in helping Plum."

What he was saying was perfectly reasonable, and Taylor knew it. Still, she couldn't stop staring at him with an injured expression. He didn't think she could win the event, and he would be working with Plum to make sure she didn't.

It didn't endear him to her. In fact, maybe Travis had been right about Eric all along.

She'd show him who couldn't win the event! "All right. Well, I have to get back to my lesson," Taylor said, now more determined to win the event than ever before.

# Chapter 14

By the time Taylor got home that evening, her every muscle ached. She and Mercedes had worked for another three hours after her fall — and clearly it showed, because as soon as she walked into the kitchen where her mother and Claire were having some tea, Jennifer stood. "Taylor, what happened to you?" she cried in alarm.

Turning to look at her reflection in the window, Taylor burst into laughter. She was filthy from head to toe, the dirt on her face streaked in patterns of sweat. Her ponytail had somehow been swept to the side and jutted out at a right angle from her head. Her jeans were split open on the side seam, a result of her fall. Her left cheek was scraped, also from the fall.

"I do look pretty bad," she had to agree.

"What happened?" Claire echoed Jennifer's question.

"My first jumping lesson."

Jennifer's eyes narrowed suspiciously. "Did you fall again?"

Taylor hesitated, not wanting her mother to worry, but also not happy about lying.

"You did, didn't you?" Jennifer insisted, hurrying to Taylor's side. "What hurts? Maybe we should go to the emergency room."

"Nothing hurts," Taylor said. This wasn't one hundred percent true. Her butt *really* hurt! She didn't think it was anything she needed to see a doctor about, though. It was just sore because she'd fallen — and then continued to ride — on it.

"Are you sure?" Jennifer asked. "Do you want some ice?"

"In a soda," Taylor suggested. "But I don't need to put ice on anything else. I'm starved. What's for supper?"

"Go take a shower, and I'll heat up some lasagna for you," Jennifer offered.

"Couldn't I just eat the lasagna and go to bed?" Taylor pleaded. "I'm so tired."

"*You're* tired?" Claire challenged. "We served twenty pounds of lasagna to a high school reunion while their band played retro heavy metal at top volume."

"Claire helped me with a catering job again today," Jennifer explained. "It was really difficult."

"I'm just teasing," Claire said. "Tired as I am, you look more exhausted, Taylor."

"I guess we're both tired," Taylor allowed, pulling the tangled elastic from her hair as she plunked down at the kitchen table. "Ow!" she complained with a wince when her butt hit the chair.

"How's Spots doing?" Claire asked.

"Doing well. Getting a little fatter every day," Taylor reported. "Will the deer sanctuary take her yet?"

When the vet had come to look over the horses at Wildwood, she had determined that Spots was a baby doe.

"They want every spot gone," Claire said. "They can't take any babies."

"Good," Taylor said. "I don't want her to go. Don't you think she could live at Wildwood?"

"No. She's a female whitetail. She needs to be around other deer."

"Aren't horses kind of the same thing as deer?" Taylor pressed.

"Not to a deer."

"Couldn't we just let her go back into the forest?"

Claire shook her head. "Spots will never be domesticated, but she's not wild anymore, either. If we kept her at Wildwood, at some point she'd jump the fence and get out, but she wouldn't have the skills to survive in the wild."

The microwave beeped, and a minute later Jennifer put a plate of heated lasagna in front of Taylor.

"So, Mom, I jumped today," Taylor announced as she dug in.

"Oh, I completely forgot to ask!" Jennifer said. "That's great! Was it hard to do?" She turned toward Claire. "The idea of Taylor jumping scares me out of my wits, but just the same, it must be thrilling."

"It was thrilling," Taylor agreed. "That's just the right word for it. It was like flying."

"Was it hard?" Jennifer asked again.

"At first it was," Taylor admitted. "But after I fe —" Taylor caught herself, but too late.

"I knew it!" Jennifer cried. "I knew you fell off!"

"But I'm fine," Taylor insisted. "Stop fussing over me. I'm not a baby!"

"Are you sure you're all right?" Jennifer asked.

"Yes!"

"Okay . . . okay. Eat your lasagna."

Taylor put another forkful into her mouth and chewed. "Anyway, I was saying," she spoke again when she was done, "I finally made it over the crossbars and landed smoothly on the other side the way Mercedes wanted me to. She's going to raise the bars a little tomorrow."

"Does her mother know that she's still spending her free time at Wildwood?" Claire asked.

"Not yet," Taylor admitted.

"Any more talk about her mother suing the ranch?" Jennifer asked.

"I don't know. Mrs. LeFleur hasn't told me any more about it. I feel weird asking Mercedes again."

"She really shouldn't sneak behind her mother's back," Jennifer commented uneasily.

"It's not like she's doing anything wrong or bad," Taylor said, reminding her mother of what she'd said in the first place.

"But it's been going on a while now, and she's lying to her mother," Jennifer pointed out.

"It's not really lying. I think she just doesn't mention it," Taylor replied.

"It comes to the same thing," Claire put in.

"I suppose," Taylor agreed, knowing deep down that Claire was right.

Taylor's cell phone rang, and she saw it was Travis. "Hang on a minute," she said to him after clicking the call through. She covered the phone and spoke to Jennifer. "Can I eat in my room?"

"No."

"In front of the TV, then, if I use a TV table?" Taylor negotiated.

"Oh, all right. Make sure you bring your plate to the kitchen when you're done," Jennifer gave in.

Taylor brought her phone and her plate into the living room and settled onto the couch with a small, collapsible table in front of her. "I jumped today!" she told Travis.

"Awesome!" he shouted. "I never thought you'd be able to do it."

Taylor wasn't sure she liked that. "Why not?"

"It just seems really hard," Travis explained.

"But if other people can do it, why would you think I couldn't?"

"You like Western. English riding just isn't you."

"It could be me," Taylor insisted. They'd had this argument before.

"Naw!"

"I would look good in an English riding outfit," Taylor maintained, feeling insulted.

On the other end of the call, Travis went into a fit of raucous laughter.

"What's so funny?" Taylor demanded.

"I'm picturing you in one of those English outfits looking all girly with your hair in a net. It's too funny."

"Why is it funny for me to be girl?" Taylor asked, annoyance in her voice. "I *am* a girl, after all."

Travis guffawed at this. "You are not!"

Taylor's jaw dropped indignantly. "I am *so!*"

"Not a *girly* girl, I mean."

"Well, no," Taylor admitted, pouting.

"Anyway, I can't picture you in that outfit, is all."

"Well, I can," Taylor said.

Travis changed the subject by telling her about a new series of Marvel comics that would be coming out soon. Taylor wasn't really listening, though. Her mind was still on the English riding outfit. She would probably need one if she was going to enter the competition.

Where would she ever get the money for that?

Taylor's phone buzzed, and she saw that someone else was calling her.

It was Eric.

Annoyed as she was at Eric, Taylor still felt a skip of excitement at the sight of his name on her phone's caller ID. "I have another call coming, Travis," she said. "I'll see you on the bus tomorrow, okay?"

"Okay. See ya."

The moment Travis clicked off, she took Eric's call. "I talked to Plum," he said right away, without even saying hi. "I convinced her to compete in a higher jumping class. It wasn't easy, but she finally agreed."

"Thanks," Taylor replied. Had he done this for her? It seemed that way. "Thanks a lot."

"Yeah, well . . . I felt kinda bad today. The stuff I was saying kept coming out wrong. I'm sure you'll be a great jumper."

"I finally landed a really clean jump after you left," Taylor told him.

"Congratulations."

"Thanks."

There was an awkward silence that Eric finally broke. "Okay, so . . . I just wanted to tell you that . . . about Plum."

"That was nice of you to do."

"So, are we friends again?" he asked a bit nervously.

"Definitely," Taylor answered. "Definitely friends."

# Chapter 15

Over the next ten days, Taylor worked with Mercedes every afternoon. When Daphne had the time, she also came to the ranch to help. By the end of that time, Taylor was taking low jumps with ease.

Finally, November fifth arrived. Taylor had arrived at the stable at six-thirty in the morning to get Prince Albert ready to be trailered to Ross River Ranch along with Shafir.

Taylor knew that Daphne's father had come earlier with a small trailer to bring Mandy over to Ross River so Daphne could compete in one of the advanced jumper events. By the time Taylor got to the ranch, Mandy was already out of her stable and gone. Taylor wished she had seen Daphne in her full riding attire. She was sure Daphne must have looked gorgeous, and she couldn't wait to see her over at Ross River Ranch.

Standing by the large trailer that Mrs. LeFleur had borrowed from Ralph Westheimer, Taylor stroked Prince Albert's neck as she crooned to him, "It's just a short trip. You'll be fine. Don't let Shafir bother you or steal all your hay while you're in there!"

As usual, Prince Albert responded to her voice, pitching his head up and neighing. He seemed to sense the excitement in the air.

Holding the side straps of his halter, Taylor walked forward up the ramp toward the open trailer door. Prince Albert came along easily. He had always been good with loading and unloading from trailers — someone had obviously trained him. Prince Albert's ease was also in part natural; he was just a calm, gentle horse.

Taylor walked Prince Albert into the trailer. Attaching the cross ties to Prince Albert's halter and making sure they were long enough so that he could reach the hay that was hanging from a net in front of them, Taylor gave her horse one last pat on the neck before walking out the side door.

The clatter of hooves on cement sounded from the main stable building, followed by a shout and the sound of a smack of flesh on flesh. Taylor hurried toward the sound, peering inside.

"You stupid horse!" Plum shouted at Shafir as she yanked sharply down on the shank chain that lay across the Arabian's nose. Shafir snorted and pulled her head up even higher to get out of reach of Plum, backing up toward the rear of the stable. Again, Plum cranked down on the chain, attempting to force Shafir to submit.

Taylor winced, watching the struggle. "Don't you think maybe you should go easy with the shank chain? Shafir has been getting really head shy lately," Taylor pointed out cautiously. She forced herself to speak calmly, not wanting to make Shafir any more stressed than she clearly was already.

Plum glowered at Taylor. "Don't you think you should mind your own business? I just tried to load her into the trailer, and she won't cooperate," Plum stated stiffly.

"Maybe it's because you keep smacking her around instead of rewarding her when she does something good!" Taylor shot back in Shafir's defense, this time forgetting to stay calm.

"Girls, girls! Enough!" Mrs. LeFleur scolded, coming out of the office. She was dressed in barn boots, jeans, and a new jacket. She'd applied an extra amount of makeup and smelled more flowery than usual. "Can we just get to this show and back without you two strangling each other?" Mrs. LeFleur requested. "Plum, give me Shafir. We don't have time for this. We're going to be late for registration."

Plum scowled at Taylor and reluctantly handed over the lead line to Mrs. LeFleur. Mrs. LeFleur undid the chain across Shafir's nose. Giving the horse a quick pat, she clipped the chain to the bottom of Shafir's halter and began walking toward the trailer.

"Plum, go grab a bucket of grain," Mrs. LeFleur instructed as she went. "Shafir will probably walk on after that if you go in first and hold it."

While Plum stalked off to the feed room to get the bucket, Taylor hurried forward to catch up with Mrs. LeFleur. "Do you see the way she uses the shank chain on Shafir?" she said quietly. "It's horrible! No wonder Shafir acts up!"

Mrs. LeFleur hushed Taylor. "I agree, but you know

how Plum gets. Now let's just load these horses on the trailer so we can go to the show."

Taylor nodded and walked back to the office to gather her show clothing. Daphne had loaned her some old show attire that no longer fit. They were slightly used, but Taylor didn't mind. Just to finally look like the sleek models in the equestrian magazines was enough, even if her tan breeches had a few stains on them.

As Taylor came out of the office, Plum was striding forward with the bucket of grain held in front of her. She clipped Taylor's shoulder as she turned, not stopping to look back, nose in the air.

Taylor spun around to shout something at Plum but caught Mrs. LeFleur's pleading look and held her words. As she hurried toward the trailer, she heard the sound of Shafir walking into it. Taylor chuckled to herself. *Great thing about horses. They'll do anything for food*, she thought.

There was a loud honk from outside. Mrs. LeFleur was driving Ralph Westheimer's rusty old blue pickup truck.

Perched there in the truck's cab, she looked even more petite than she already was.

The trailer was attached to the back of the truck, and Taylor could see the horses' tails swish as they munched on their hay. She hurried to the truck, hopping in next to Plum. Plum scowled and moved her garment, boot, and helmet bags over so Taylor could fit. Taylor's gaze lingered on the expensive-looking garment bag, which no doubt held Tailored Sportsman breeches and jackets.

Plum *had* been riding for a long time, but at least they wouldn't be in the same class at the show today. She knew Plum would be a tough competitor in the ring, and she probably couldn't beat her. Taylor thought again how she had Eric to thank for the fact that Plum wouldn't be competing against her.

The sun was just rising as they wound their way through Pheasant Valley. "Horse shows require early mornings and long days," Mrs. LeFleur remarked.

Taylor peered out the window, watching trees and houses go by on the winding back roads. Although Pheasant Valley often seemed dull to Taylor, she did appreciate the beauty of it. As they got closer to Ross River Ranch, she noticed a distinct change in the houses.

They were larger and more grand, often with wrought-iron gates. She could see gleaming chandeliers inside of some of the houses and imagined what it would be like to go into one of them.

The skies began to change from the early morning pinks and oranges to the lighter azure blue of day. They approached a winding gravel road, with a huge sign that said ROSS RIVER RANCH in cursive writing.

Taylor had been to Ross River two times before, once with Daphne, who used to board Mandy there, and another time when she helped her mother cater a luncheon at Mrs. Ross's private home, which was on the ranch grounds. Still, though she'd seen it before, Taylor couldn't help but be impressed as they went down the road, past large green fields with white wood railings. *Ross River Ranch looks like something out of a movie*, Taylor thought as they pulled up and saw in front of them a large number of trailers and trucks, with people milling about.

The barn itself was white with a deep red trim, contrasting beautifully with the well-manicured green fields around it. There was a large ring to the left of the barn, where riders were warming up and practicing their jumps.

Mrs. LeFleur took the key from the ignition and turned to the girls. "Are you ready, ladies? Don't be nervous, this is just a local show, nothing super fancy or rated. I bet you'll both do great."

Despite her speech, Mrs. LeFleur looked like *she* was the one who needed a pep talk. Her hands were tight on the steering wheel, and her shoulders were tense as she stared at the barn in front of them. *It must be hard for her,* Taylor thought, *having not been here for so many years and facing the possibility of seeing Mrs. Ross again.*

"What do I have to be nervous about?" Plum scoffed. "I always win these small local competitions. No one very good competes, anyway. It's more like practice for me."

Taylor scowled. This was her first competition ever, and she thought it was plenty intimidating.

"Well, I'm glad you're feeling so confident, Plum," Mrs. LeFleur said, not looking at her. "Let's unload these horses and go sign in."

They got the horses out of the trailer and brought them down to the registration booth, which was located in between the barn and the ring. Mrs. LeFleur went ahead to register the girls and the horses for their various classes. Taylor looked over to the ring to see who was warming up and noticed Daphne flying gracefully over the jumps on top of Mandy. Daphne and Mandy were so elegant over jumps, Taylor couldn't help but aspire to be like them one day.

After finishing the last jump, Daphne glanced over and noticed Taylor waving. She smiled and waved back, dismounting and walking over to them. "Hey, how's it going?" she asked.

"So far so good," Taylor replied with, hearing the nervous tremor in her own voice. "Is Mercedes here?"

"She should be around here somewhere," Daphne said. "My dad picked her up this morning. I guess she's your coach for today. She keeps looking around inside the barn for something, but I'm not sure what."

"She's so secretive sometimes," Taylor commented.

"I know," Daphne said with a shrug. "I have to go cool off and untack Mandy, but I'll be around. Let me know if you need me."

Daphne was competing in one of the highest levels of the show, the jumper class. Its courses always looked intimidating to Taylor. Daphne had explained that the jumper class was a timed event, where riders tried to complete a course as quickly and as precisely as they could.

There were penalties if a horse knocked over a jump or refused to jump. The jumps were higher and more intertwined, making the course harder to memorize.

Taylor waved good-bye as Daphne walked away with Mandy, then she turned to Prince Albert, who was looking around at the new scenery and all the people. "All right, boy. Let's go get you groomed up and show-ready!"

Taylor returned to the trailer and clipped Prince Albert to the side, placing some hay for him to munch on as she groomed him. On the other side of the trailer, Plum was grooming Shafir.

Every once in a while there would be the sound of a smack and a shrill whinny from the opposite side. Taylor flinched each time, wanting to stop Plum, but knowing that the girl wouldn't change her behavior. Shafir was probably playing with a curry comb or hoof pick in Plum's back pocket, which resulted in a smack from Plum.

Mercedes suddenly appeared, walking toward the trailer. She somehow didn't seem very excited to be there.

Taylor waved happily, but Mercedes only gave a jerk of her chin in greeting. What was wrong?

As Mercedes approached, Taylor put down the brush she was holding. "Hey, are you all right?" Taylor asked.

"Yeah. Fine," Mercedes said flatly.

"Are you sure you're feeling okay?"

"I'm fine. Drop it." Mercedes said, finally looking Taylor in the eyes. "So, are you excited about your first show? Don't let me down. We've trained too hard for you to mess this up."

"Excited *and* nervous. I think I'll be okay, though."

"You're lucky you have a good horse to ride," Mercedes said, gazing toward Prince Albert but seeming lost in her own thoughts.

"Maybe you should have competed," Taylor said, thinking that might be what was bothering Mercedes. "I know you don't have your own horse, but . . ." Taylor trailed off as she saw Mercedes' eyes brim with tears.

*Uh-oh.* Why was Mercedes suddenly crying? It wasn't like her. Something really bad must have happened.

Mercedes turned away from Taylor, walking a few feet away. Taylor hurried after her, putting a hand on her shoulder, but Mercedes flinched away from the touch.

"You know, you can tell me if something is bothering you. I won't tell anyone," Taylor said softly.

Mercedes whipped around to face Taylor, tears streaking her face. "You want to know what's bothering me?

Really? Come on." Turning, Mercedes walked quickly toward the barn.

Not sure what to do, Taylor looked back and forth between Mercedes and Prince Albert. "Can you keep an eye on Prince Albert for me?" she shouted to Plum. "I have something I have to go do!"

"Yeah, fine, whatever," Plum shouted back.

"Thanks!" Taylor called back, now jogging behind Mercedes, who was already halfway to the barn. "What do you have to show me?" she asked as she caught up.

Mercedes stopped walking and turned on her heel. Taylor was hurrying so closely behind, she almost collided with her. "My horse," Mercedes said.

"You have a horse?" Taylor replied, confused.

*"Had."*

"Had?"

"Had."

# Chapter 16

ust follow me," Mercedes said, moving into the front of the Ross River barn. She turned to the right and walked purposefully down an aisle. The barn was astoundingly clean, with high ceilings and not a trace of dirt. Although Taylor had seen it when she came with Daphne, she still marveled at how tidy this barn was, each large wooden stall bearing its own bronzed name plaque.

Mercedes stopped at the last stall on the left and pointed to a gleaming white horse that lifted its head upon her arrival.

"This horse is yours?" Taylor murmured, looking at the gelding's strong body and shining coat.

"Was!" Mercedes shouted impatiently, then sighed and said softly, "I told you. I don't own him anymore."

Taylor nodded and looked back and forth between the two of them.

"He's really gorgeous. What's his name?" Taylor asked.

"His registered name is Montana Wind Dancer. His barn name was Monty when I owned him."

"*He's* Monty?!" Taylor cried.

"Yep. I told you he was some guy I used to like," Mercedes confirmed. "I really, *really* liked him," she added, her voice cracking. She opened the latch to the door and walked in, petting Monty softly.

"When did you own him?" Taylor asked.

"Back when I lived in Connecticut," Mercedes replied, looking wistfully at Monty. "My dad bought him for me for my thirteenth birthday from a Missouri Fox Trotting breeder. Like I told you, we had our own stable, so I could ride him all the time. He's a great horse. Does jumps, trails, dressage, everything."

"So why did you get rid of him?" Taylor questioned, approaching the stall and leaning on the wooden frame.

"I had to. We couldn't afford him anymore," Mercedes

said quietly, looking down. "My dad was working on Wall Street in the stock market and ended up getting involved with some bad deals. When the economy started turning for the worse and the stock market started going down" — she sighed again — "the first thing to go was Monty."

Mercedes wrapped her arms around the white horse, burying her face into his shoulder. "And then the cars. And then the house." Her shoulders moved up and down as she quietly cried into Monty's coat. Taylor stepped forward, putting a comforting hand on her shoulder.

"So we had to sell him to some person who owned another barn in Connecticut. He bought Monty and a bunch of the other horses from us. He gave Monty to his niece, who lives around here. I e-mailed him a while ago to see how Monty was and found out they'd sold Monty and a few others to Ross River Ranch. I was happy to hear Monty was nearby, but you know how this place is; you can't just come and visit without permission. The only reason I can be here today is because they're having this open show. It's the real reason I didn't want to compete. If I couldn't compete on Monty, I didn't want to do it at all."

Taylor watched as Mercedes stroked the horse's soft neck. Monty seemed to respond to Mercedes as if he knew her and missed her. He nickered softly and nudged her chest gently. Mercedes chuckled and grinned through her tears. Reaching into her back pocket, she produced a sugar cube. Monty stretched his neck forward and licked up the small, sweet block. Taylor had never seen this soft side of Mercedes.

Suddenly, an idea hit Taylor. "Mercedes! I've got it! I know how we can get you here to see Monty more!"

"What? How?" Mercedes asked, eyes alert.

"The winner of each class gets five free lessons here!" Taylor said excitedly. "If I can get first place, you could come with me and visit!"

"You're right! I think you could win it, too! You've gotten really good, even though we haven't had much time to teach you," Mercedes said with enthusiasm.

Taylor looked down at the time on her watch and jumped. "I've got to go! I still have to tack up Prince Albert and put on the show clothes Daphne gave me. And my class starts in twenty minutes!" she shouted, turning and walking quickly back toward the trailer.

"Right — go get 'em! I'll be standing at the side of the ring to help coach you," Mercedes replied, her tears now gone.

Taylor hurried away. She rushed back to the trailer, to find Plum perched on the bed of the truck, munching on a sandwich.

"You're going to be late," Plum said, looking down at Taylor.

"No, I'm not," Taylor said, grabbing the saddle pad, saddle, and girth from the trailer. She tacked up Prince Albert quicker than she ever had before. Grabbing a hoof pick from the grooming cart, she ran her hand down his back right leg.

"C'mon, boy. Pick up your leg. One last clean." Then Taylor stopped and gasped, "Prince Albert! No! Where did your shoe go?"

Plum glanced down from her perch, brows raised and a smirk on her face. "Really? You didn't check his hoofs before putting him on the trailer? What a rookie move."

"What am I going to do? He can't jump if he's missing a back shoe! I knew it was a little loose, but I thought it'd stay on! And my class is in" — she glanced at her watch again — "fifteen minutes!"

"Guess you're out of luck," Plum said, hopping down from the truck. She grabbed her helmet and twisted her blonde hair under the cap. "I'll just have to win this class without any competition."

Taylor stopped, midpanic. "Wait, you're in this class? Isn't this class for beginners? Eric told me you weren't riding in it."

"I just told him that so he'd stop bugging me about it," Plum said, sliding out of the truck. "But I thought it'd be amusing to ride in the same class as you. Just because."

So Taylor had been right — Plum knew she was a more advanced rider and decided to join the beginners just to make sure Taylor didn't win.

Plum put Shafir's bridle on, yanking her forward.

Taylor's lower lip began to quiver. What was she going to do? It was hopeless now! She sighed and slumped down next to Prince Albert, feeling defeated. Why even bother to compete?

Just then, Mercedes came running up. "Your class is going on, like, now!" she shouted, motioning for Taylor to hurry.

"I can't go. Prince Albert threw his back shoe. He can't do a jump course like this," Taylor moaned, standing up and walking toward Mercedes.

"Seriously? Oh, no!" Mercedes cried.

The girls stared at each other for a moment.

"Do they have farriers at events like these?" Taylor asked. "Maybe we could get a new shoe put on."

"There's no time for that now," Mercedes reminded her. Then Mercedes' eyes narrowed, and her face took on a determined expression. "No. You're not going to lose this chance. We're going to use Monty."

Taylor stared at her, dumbfounded. "We're not allowed to just ride him, are we?"

"I don't care. It's a Ross River event — let them supply you with one of their horses," Mercedes insisted. "And anyone riding Monty is a surefire first place!"

Taylor looked nervously to the barn where Monty was. "I mean, I guess. If *you* think it's a good idea," she said, still not sure this was the right thing to do.

Mercedes nodded emphatically. "Go untack Prince Albert, and meet me at Monty's stall. I'll get him groomed and ready. Hurry up!"

Just as quickly as Taylor had tacked Prince Albert, she

untacked him with lightning speed. Prince Albert stood there, ears perked, noticing the commotion. Taylor grabbed the saddle and started running toward the barn, then stopped and turned around, looking at Prince Albert.

"Sorry, boy. It's for your own safety that you don't go over jumps missing a shoe," she apologized. Then she hurried off to the barn to tack up Monty and change into her show clothing.

Within minutes, Monty was ready to go. He was a magnificent sight, with his gleaming white coat and thick muscles. Mercedes and Taylor hurried to the entrance gate just in time to see Plum beginning her course.

# Chapter 17

Shafir snorted and pulled at the reins. Plum held a riding crop in her right hand and began her courtesy circle, picking up a canter. Shafir raced forward, eager to run, but Plum yanked back hard on the reins. Tossing her head in the air, Shafir playfully pranced toward the first jump.

Plum jerked the reins back again. Raising her right hand, she brought the riding crop down on Shafir's side.

From outside the ring where they waited with Monty, Taylor and Mercedes held their breath as they watched Plum. Taylor gave Mercedes a sidelong glance, not needing words to convey what they were both thinking: Plum's ride was getting dangerous.

Shafir raced forward toward the jump once again, leaping over it. Plum clung on, clearly not ready for such an unexpected leap. She landed awkwardly but stayed on. The audience could hear her growling and muttering at her horse as she careened around the ring toward the second jump. At the last moment, Shafir ducked out and headed for the jump next to the one Plum was aiming for.

Pulling hard to the right, Plum attempted to drag Shafir back on course, but it was too late. Shafir had plans of her own. Jumping too low this time caused two of the poles to come tumbling down underneath them as the Arabian stumbled forward.

Taylor and Mercedes exchanged another look, this time one of excitement. Knocking down poles meant point deductions, and better yet, going off course meant the rider was disqualified! They turned their heads back to the ring just in time to see Shafir stop right in front of the third jump, sending Plum sailing forward.

The crowd gasped as Plum hurtled into the jump, knocking all the poles down with a crash!

Shafir pranced backward and began trotting around the arena, looking happy to be free of her rider. Plum stood up, shaken but not too hurt. Covered in dirt, she ripped off her helmet and threw it on the ground. She chucked her riding crop toward the outside of the ring. Finally, she stormed out, passing Mercedes and Taylor without glancing up.

"You've got this," Mercedes said to Taylor. "Monty is a very simple ride, just be sure to give him gentle and clear commands. He loves to jump. I guess I'll go grab Shafir now," she added, opening the gate and hurrying toward the excited horse.

Taylor nodded, clipping her helmet underneath her chin. Placing her left foot in Monty's stirrup, she hoisted herself up and onto the saddle. She shifted about in the tack. Everything seemed a lot higher up here; Monty was at least a hand taller than Prince Albert.

Taylor took a deep breath and reached forward, stroking Monty's neck. "Hope you're as good as Mercedes says you are," she whispered to the gelding.

Straightening up, she pushed her heels down and shoulders back, ready to enter the arena. Mercedes finally captured Shafir. She gave Taylor a reassuring wink as she brought the Arabian out through the gate.

"Now entering the arena is number 942, Taylor Henry,

riding Prince Albert," the announcer said over the loud-speakers. Taylor frowned. Would they find out that this wasn't the horse she registered with? Would they care?

Now wasn't the time to think about it. She took a deep breath and held her chin high, like Mercedes had instructed her.

As she began her opening circle, picking up the canter, she began to see what Mercedes was talking about. Monty had an incredibly smooth gate, almost more so than Prince Albert. Her confidence grew as she raised herself into two-point, sending Monty sailing over the first jump, clearing it with ease. She looked to her second jump, and once more, Monty eagerly leaped over. All Taylor had to do was direct him where to go, and Monty took each jump like a champion show horse, picking his knees up high, ears perked forward, and landing with grace. Before Taylor knew it, she had completed the course and nodded to the judge, signaling that she was finished.

She looked about frantically for Mercedes as she left the arena, thumping Monty on the neck, giving him congratulatory pats. She hoped Mercedes had seen them! Mrs. LeFleur stood off to the side of the ring, looking baffled and holding Shafir.

Suddenly, Mercedes came hurtling toward Taylor and Monty.

"You did it! That was a completely clean course! There's no *way* anyone could beat you!"

Taylor had barely dismounted before Mercedes grabbed her in a joyful embrace.

"Monty did it! I just sat there and told him where to go!" Taylor replied with a laugh as Mercedes moved to wrap her arms around Monty, snuggling into his soft mane.

"They're going to be announcing the placing soon. You were the last to ride," Mercedes said, handing the reins back to Taylor. "Go back in there!"

All the competitors entered the arena again, some still on top of their horses, some standing next to them. Taylor looked at the other girls. They were dressed so nicely, and all of their horses were beautiful. She wished she had seen them ride so she could gauge how she had done in comparison. All she could do now was hope.

The announcer began listing off places, starting with sixth. There were nine riders in total, which meant three people wouldn't even get a ribbon. As the number of riders dwindled, Taylor began to get nervous. Her number hadn't been called yet, which could either mean she didn't get a ribbon or it could mean . . .

". . . And in first place, winning the blue ribbon and five free riding lessons here at the beautiful Ross River Ranch, is . . ." The announcer paused. Taylor held her breath and looked at the ground, eyes squeezed shut.

"Number 942, Taylor Henry, riding Prince Albert!"

Taylor leaped in the air, startling Monty just slightly.

"Yes!" she shouted.

Mercedes raced into the ring and gave Taylor a bear hug, nearly squeezing all the air out of her. "You did it, you did it! I told you that you could do it!" she cried, dancing around.

A girl with a blue ribbon strode forward, placing it on Monty's cheek piece. It looked perfect against his fine white coat.

Everyone began exiting the ring, but Taylor couldn't move — or stop grinning.

Her first show was a great success! She had done it!

"I'd better get Monty back before anyone realizes he's gone," Mercedes said. "Would you mind if I ride him back, just for — you know — old times?"

"Sure, go ahead. I'll meet you at the trailer, and we'll see Daphne's event." Taylor smiled as Mercedes hopped into Monty's saddle and handed Taylor the blue ribbon.

When they were a distance away, Taylor broke into a run, racing down a grassy slope toward the trailer to find Prince Albert who was still hitched there.

"We did it, boy! I won, but I couldn't have done it if you hadn't helped me."

Taylor wrapped her arms around Prince Albert's neck, pressing her forehead into his skin. She loved him so much! Thinking of Mercedes and Monty, she shut her eyes and made a silent promise. No matter what the future might hold, she'd never let anyone or anything take Prince Albert away from her.

# Come back to

## WILDWOOD STABLES

## Stealing the Prize

Turn the page for a sneak peek!

Diagonals!" shouted a male voice from the gate.

Taylor snapped out of her daydream and looked to where the voice had come from. A short, skinny man, dressed neatly in a dark blue baseball cap that read USEF, stood at the entrance to the ring. White tufts of hair were visible from under his cap and his thick, gray eyebrows were raised, making his forehead crinkle, as he watched Taylor ride. He wore a simple black T-shirt and the customary tan breeches and polished black tall boots of an English style rider.

Diagonals gave Taylor more trouble than any other part of English riding. It was so difficult to tell which of the horse's front legs was swinging forward without looking! She broke Monty down to a walk and moved toward the man, suddenly much tenser than she was before. "Hi, my name is Taylor," she said when she was close to him. "Are you my instructor?"

"Keith Hobbes," he responded, touching the brim of his cap in greeting. "Now, go pick up the correct diagonal. Do a warm-up lap."

Taylor obeyed, guiding Monty over to the rail. She glanced down to Monty's outside leg, rising up out of the saddle as it came forward. *Wow, he doesn't waste any time*, Taylor thought as she tried to keep the up-down rhythm.

"Close your hip angle," Keith called out. Taylor was glad that he didn't seem as annoyed and hurried as Mercedes often did. "You're a Western rider, aren't you?" he observed.

"Does it still show?" she asked, chagrined. Taylor wanted to believe that she was moving back and forth between the two styles with grace. She had first learned Western style when she was around eight, but now that she wanted to jump, she had to learn English. There was no jumping in Western riding.

"Yep. It shows a little," he replied. Taylor bent forward at her hip, trying to mask her Western riding background as best she could. Since Western riders generally learned to sit on their back pockets, she had to relearn and practice being more perched in the saddle.

"We're going to work on your English riding form a bit today. Okay?" Keith's voice rang through the ring, calm and instructional. "Now, I want you to bring your lower leg back and push more weight into your heels," he said.

Taylor tried to do both, all the while keeping the posting trot. "Good. Much better!" Keith praised her.

Taylor smiled at his encouraging words. Mercedes almost never gave her any positive reinforcement. Mercedes wasn't *mean* and Taylor was grateful for the instruction she was giving her, but the girl had a bossy, critical streak that could be hard to take. It was just nice to hear a compliment for a change.

"I want to see more bend in your arm. Now, ask for a canter," Keith instructed, as Taylor sat down and nudged Monty into the quicker, three-beat gate. "Check your lead! Is it correct?" Keith stood with his arms folded and watched Taylor move around the ring.

She broke Monty back into the trot. "I guess not? Uh . . . sorry . . . but what's a lead?" Taylor asked, feeling uninformed and embarrassed. He probably expected his rider would know these things already. Had she disappointed him on their very first lesson?

## You belong at
# WILDWOOD STABLES

Friendship, rivalry, and the amazing place that
brings them together . . . Read them all!

#1: Daring to Dream

#2: Playing for Keeps

#3: Racing Against Time

#4: Learning to Fly

#5: Stealing the Prize